THE LAST RHINO

AN AFRICAN WILDLIFE ADVENTURE

DAVID MARK QUIGLEY

Published by Hashbooks Publishing
Copyright © 2021 David Mark Quigley All rights reserved.

The characters and events portrayed in this book are fictitious. Any similarity to real persons, living or dead, is coincidental and not intended by the author.

No part of this book may be reproduced, or stored in a retrieval system, or transmitted in any form or by any means, electronic, mechanical, photocopying, recording, or otherwise, without express written permission of the author.

Paperback ISBN-13: 978-1-955388-15-3

First Edition Published 2021

The Last Rhino is dedicated to my friend and colleague Hal Tapley. I have always enjoyed the ease with which we communicate, your steadying hand, and the wisdom of your advice. Thank you for being a great friend and all your support over the years.

*"Innocence, once lost, can never be regained.
Darkness, once gazed upon, can never be lost"*

– John Milton

AUTHOR NOTE

The events in this story take place just prior to the start of *White Gold*, book 2 in my African series, and are loosely based on Tony Campbell's rhino anti-poaching efforts.

The Last Rhino is a novella, about a 40,000 words, and prequel to *White Gold* in my African series, which can be read and enjoyed in any order. I've made sure not to include spoilers for those of you who are new to my works and any existing fans will still find plenty of fresh action and intrigue, as well as a little detail of Tony, his background and some of the players in his world.

I loved revisiting Tony's life again, and had an absolute blast writing this book. I hope you have as much enjoyment reading it too.

David Mark Quigley

PROLOGUE

Night Feeder: Zambezi Valley, Zimbabwe

IT WAS DARK and quiet. So quiet he could hear the tigertail dragonflies thrumming. He stood beside a copse of mopane trees, just off a well-used game trail, listening. In front of him was the mighty Zambezi River, tumbling, like distant rolling thunder, endlessly down towards the Indian Ocean. At this time of the night, he would have silently walked down the game trail to the river's edge and drank. But not tonight. Instinct warned him trouble was not too far away. It was the lack of noise that had disrupted his nightly routine. He could still easily hear the river, but there was no chorus of crickets, shovel-nosed or sand frogs in song. Something had definitely disturbed these usual nocturnal sounds.

He tentatively stepped out of the trees and turned, his nostrils quivering, sniffing the air, and vanished into a thick maze of scrubland.

He didn't like it, and although his eyesight was weak, with this impenetrable African darkness it made no difference. Like a blind man, he knew the run of this area of the Zambezi Valley by sense of smell and touch alone. He could easily navigate this rugged bush-strewn valley through the hidden pathways and trails without being seen or heard; only when he wanted to be. At 3,000 pounds, 12-feet long and six-feet tall at the shoulder, this alone was a remarkable feat. But as he was the last of the great horned, hook-lipped black rhinoceroses of this valley, it was what had kept him alive.

Mistakenly perceived as one of the most stupid, cantankerous, nervously inquisitive game in all of Africa, he had drawn from the benefit of millions of years of evolution, passed down through his lineage from his great ancestors the perissodactyls, who were the forefathers of other highly intelligent species, like the zebra and the horse. He had adapted and, using his incredible intellect, developed a uniquely perceptive cunning and survived. Normally seen as an animal that charges anything that provokes its wrath, this particular male was different. He was literally an anomaly. After seeing so many of his family and kind killed and maimed it had triggered something deep within his brain. He had become secretive and stealthy as he moved amongst the jesse bush, a thick scrubland, that now made up his home.

Born as a twin and weighing far less than his male sibling, from the first day of his birth he had to adapt to survive. He became tenacious and resilient, and had to use his intellect to get his fair share of his mother's milk before he and his sibling were weaned. At times he succeeded, while at others he was bullied and deprived. He quickly learnt what worked and what didn't. Even before he was weaned he followed his mother's lead and began to browse, eating those succulent shoots, leaves and fruits that were found deep in the woodlands and jesse bush of the Zambezi Valley.

Before he had reached 18 months old, he was already getting the bulk of his food from the plants of his valley. Luckily for him he had developed this early independent spirit and adaptability. One day, at the start of his second rainy season, he learnt the harsh reality that faced his kind. He had wandered off on his own, a little further from his mother and twin, as he had now grown accustomed to doing, browsing, taking advantage of the new growth that followed the rain. He already weighed close to 600 pounds, and was steadily growing in size each day. As he was stripping the succulent green foliage from bushes and snapping off low acacia branches, he was jolted out of his feasting reverie. A harsh noise of crashing barks, like thunder, spooked him and sent him tearing away in fear through the bush.

After many hours, crying out for his family with high-pitched screams, he made his way back to where he had last seen them. Only to find blood-soaked carcasses beneath a buzzing halo of flies and vultures. Sending the vultures scattering, he stood beside the dismembered bodies of his mother and brother, smelling them, and wailing and mewling like an oversized kitten. They had been cut down, murdered with deep gashes on their heads, their faces hacked off and their horns gone. All around them was trampled grass and bush, reeking of an acrid scent that he soon learnt was man, a scent that he grew to fear and hate.

Left all alone to fend for himself, he gazed mournfully through his long eyelashes at the plains and woodlands, which suddenly looked vast and terrifying. His survival instincts kicked in, telling him to flee. He turned and left, never to return to this spot again.

Five years on, he adapted without his family. He had at first learnt to avoid that acrid stench, for during those years he had come upon similar scenes and instinctively knew only stealth and cunning would allow him to survive.

The first three times he had close calls with man, his only predator, had been pivotal in his understanding and now continued interaction with these hated marauders. The first, in fear, he had merged into the bush and run away, hurried on by those thunderous barking shouts that seemed to accompany these loud and obnoxious creatures. The fright and his harried flight never sat well with him, eating at his reasoning, it vexed and worried him.

But then he'd gotten wise and found another way of dealing with these hated invaders. So the next two times he was pursued, he slunk into the undergrowth, hid and silently waited.

The second time, firstly in fear, then in outrage, like an avalanche, he had attacked, exploding his bulk through the wall of bush he had hidden behind, and was surprised at how incredibly frail and easy to kill these attackers turned out to be. He impaled one, flicked him off his horn and drove a second one up and crushed him against the trunk of a jackalberry tree. He left them there and chose to avoid that spot in future.

On the third occasion, he realized with stealth, slyness and vigilance he had an edge over these adversaries. Even with his limited eyesight he intimately knew the lay of the land. This time he listened and waited, and even though he didn't recognize it as such, began to hunt them. There were three of them. One died with a horn through his kidneys when he impaled him from behind after he had walked past his place of concealment. The man had been scouting ahead on his own and had stopped to relieve himself against the base of a blackwood tree. He had emerged from his screen of bush and soundlessly walked up behind the man and dispatched him with his horn.

The second had rounded a corner on the trail the group was using and was confronted by the beast. He died a lingering death with a crushed pelvis, courtesy of a front hoof stomped onto the small of his back. The third, who threw up some sort of stick that barked flames and shouted violently in his face, died as the contents of his torso were ripped from his body by the flick and toss of his sharpened horn. He left these three invaders where they lay, but returned a day later to find their remains had been devoured by hyenas.

He had also seen others like himself snatched off the savanna and abducted by these alien invaders and locked away inside the belly of monsters with many big round, rolling black feet.

Being the dominant bull in his territory, he endlessly patrolled and had now begun to defend his domain. His fierce cunning had planted unsettling fears in the nearby villagers. For the years that followed these encounters, there was talk of witchcraft and ethereal sentinels who patrolled the valley.

There were swirling stories of men seen entering this part of the Zambezi Valley, yet never to be seen again.

He sensed rather than saw the dawn's strengthening light. It was as if the river began to awaken, its eddies and splashing undulations seemed to be getting louder. Then he heard the haunting, sing-song cry of a hunting fish eagle ringing through the valley, and a lone red-crested cuckoo echo its monotonous longing call, way off in the distance. There would be a multitude of other birds welcoming in the coming day. The sun would light up the valley bottom, the golden grass and the untamed Zambezi, its dense riverine bush, interspersed with bare quartzite boulders. Above these sculptured rocks would soon be seen the green canopy of trees, adorned with woody creepers and twisted vines, rising up the river gorge's wall to eventually give way to the changing woodlands beyond.

As the stark light of day more readily revealed his presence, it was time to go and melt his massive frame back into the dense thicket that was his domain. He had again caught the acrid odor, the stench of man, the hated enemy. These bipod destroyers were the only predator he had ever known. Almost magically he disappeared. When the nighttime darkness came, and the time was right, he would turn the tables once again and avenge his family, and his other kith and kin, his communal crash, who had been relentlessly pursued and taken from his home.

CHAPTER 1

Zambezi Valley, Zimbabwe

One late-afternoon just as the sun set over the Zambezi Valley, Tony Campbell picked up on the heart-shaped footprints of one particular rhino bull. There was little wildlife left living in this over-poached part of the valley that he patrolled. This pristine strip of wilderness was no longer the refuge it had long been thought of. Its isolation made it both perfect and perilous for wildlife. After decades of political instability, poverty and crime had risen, and so had illegal organized poaching that had left mental scars on much of its animal population.

Tony, along with a handful of rangers, was fighting to protect and restore the wildlife in his section of the Zambezi Valley. The 26-year-old, six-foot and super-athletic, with a tuft of short sandy hair framing cool blue eyes and an intelligent, chiseled face, quickly became known as one of the gutsiest conservationists in southern Africa. With his movie-star good looks, he seemed like an unlikely wildlife vigilante.

In those slow, searing hot summer days of 1987, Zimbabwe's Zambezi Valley, stretching from Mana Pools National Park in the north, to the rugged Zambezi River gorge below Victoria Falls in the southwest, had the worst wave of poaching. The remaining elephants and rhinos in the valley were as elusive as ghosts. But Tony was an adept tracker, courtesy of his rugged African upbringing. Growing up among wildlife and tribesmen, tracking and reading animal signs was just part of everyday life in the bush. He could smell and sense animals long before he saw them.

Soon Tony found the spot where the lone rhino had lain down under a lacey canopy of an acacia and the grass where he vigorously spread his dung to mark his territory. His spoor was very distinctive and marked him as an exceptionally large and healthy male. Tony knew if he could read this animal's sign, so could everyone else, friend or foe, that walked and patrolled his rugged domain. He had long known that among the last rhinos in this section of the valley there was a mother with two calves. But years ago, after his fellow rangers found her massacred along with one calf, he wondered what happened to the other one. By the time he found sign of the missing calf who miraculously survived on his own, he was fully grown. Every time he came across his spoor, he marveled at how this magnificent primeval beast had survived for so long, in what had become a no-man's-land of sorts. He reasoned it was only a matter of time before the bull succumbed to a poacher's bullet.

The quest to save this lone rhino soon became an obsession for Tony and his team.

It had taken him many months to unravel the rhino's nightly routine. The dramatic spike in poaching traffic, Tony believed, had triggered his survival instincts making him very wary and secretive, hiding by day and moving only at night to water. It was this habit that led Tony to his nighttime vigil.

Stretching between the borders of Zimbabwe and Zambia, Lake Kariba was an ecological wonderland, teeming with hippos and crocodiles and wildlife that came to drink from its emerald shores. It was at the top of the headwaters of this body of water that Tony spent most of his time.

Like most nights and usually alone, Tony sat quietly in a game hide he had sighted with care and constructed of hardwood poles, canvas screening, layered with brush. The hide's peephole and firing slot opened onto a small grass and sandy spit, close to the end of the Victoria Falls section of the Kariba Gorge on the Zimbabwean side of the river, before it flowed into the massive manmade hydroelectric Lake Kariba. He had used this technique successfully many times before. When he heard the animal come down to drink he would activate a battery-powered jacklight positioned above the hide, illuminating his prey and tranquilize the beast.

He remained on the trail of this ghost rhino and nurtured his dream of capturing him for many months. But as dawn's faint light broke over the horizon, he knew his rhino wasn't coming. Not tonight anyway. In the gauzy, grey pre-dawn, he walked back to his camp through woodlands of cathedral mopane and giant baobabs, thinking he had to beat the poaching thugs and spirit this bull to a secure sanctuary very far away.

He would be back that evening to begin the vigil all over again.

For the last few years Tony had been involved with Operation Stronghold, a government-backed rhino protection and translocation program in Zimbabwe. The operation, overseen by ZimParks, Zimbabwe Parks and Wildlife Management Authority, was funded by conservation organizations from all over the world. Tony was a leading member of a hundred-odd men that patrolled the 7,500 square miles of the Zambezi Valley and helped relocate the black rhinos from its woodlands. So far he had been involved with well over 300 relocations, helping create viable breeding populations in protected pockets throughout Zimbabwe. What had started as a conservation exercise had now turned into a bloody and brutal bush war. For Tony, who spent his life surrounded by animals he grew to love deeply, it was an intensely personal war. He was determined to fight "this incessant poaching holocaust" by whatever means necessary, and had no qualms of killing a poacher.

The Zambezi Valley was the last stronghold of one of the four sub-species of these prehistoric beasts. In the past, Zimbabwe's rhino population had been relatively stable, but those days were long gone. By the 1980s, badly administered national parks and government corruption in the north had supplied the insatiable market of the Middle East and the world's largest illicit trading center, Taiwan, with the rhinos' eagerly sought-after horn. But as these easy pickings diminished, the inevitable happened, greedy eyes focused further south on Zimbabwe.

The use of rhino horn for the handles of the Yemenis and Saudi Arabian *jambiya*, as an aphrodisiac in India, and largely the booming Asian trade in the horns for its non-existent medicinal properties decimated Africa's rhinos. The horns, composed of keratin, the same substance as hair, nails and hooves, were purported to be a cure for *everything*. A few short decades ago, the African forests were full of wild black rhinos, once numbering in the millions, by the 1980s was down to a few thousand, while the white rhinos were nearly extinct with less than a hundred individuals left.

Without elephants and rhinos, the plains, forests and savannahs would be a different and emptier place. Elephants push over trees, stamp down scrubby areas to create grazing spots while rhinos maintain the grasslands, diversifying plant life on which so many other animals depend. The loss of these keystone species, the most significant land mammals on this planet, has a ripple effect on all other animals, birds and insects. Without them, the entire ecosystem would crumble.

As the rhinos hurtled towards extinction this desperate situation had required more than just desperate measures. It had thrust Tony into a deadly mission that had turned Zimbabwe into the last stand for the wild rhino.

Following his incredible success at achieving results, Tony was coming to the end of his tenure with Operation Stronghold, having been poached by the WWF, World Wildlife Fund, to take up a new role overseeing elephant conservation in southern and eastern Africa.

Before leaving Operation Stronghold, he had to catch and relocate this one last male rhino. It was the one, if not the only, remaining rhino in one particular section of the Zambezi escarpment that had turned into the main poaching gateway, serving as a funnel that brought in the poachers and out their valuable contraband. It was this corridor where Tony spent most of his time, either combating the insurgent poaching, searching for snares and traps and trying, unsuccessfully, to capture this one last rhino.

The corridor, as it had become known, existed because of the area's location and proximity to the Kariba Gorge. It was the last area of heavily wooded river frontage that presented relatively open stretches of beach and landing spots for the Zambian poachers, before the Zambezi girth diminished, its banks became inaccessible, and the river became unnavigable. While Tony hadn't yet been able to determine the exact method the poachers used to come across the river, it was the generally accepted consensus that they navigated across the Zambezi in the dugout canoes that fishermen used on both sides of the river.

Along with the capture of this lone bull, this was another conundrum he desperately wanted to solve.

CHAPTER 2

Mana Pools National Park

'WELL, WE'RE GOING to be sorry to see you go,' Glenn Tatum, chief warden of Zimbabwe's national parks, said to Tony. A tall, thickly built bull of a man, with cropped brown hair and a curt military manner, Glenn was the driving force behind Operation Stronghold. His gun-metal grey eyes and his determined jaw marked him as a man of authority.

They sat with Andy Woodward, the lanky, long-haired head warden of Mana Pools National Park, the unofficial field headquarters for Operation Stronghold. They were lamenting his departure to the WWF's new elephant protection program. At the end of that summer, Tony would be leaving in three months in March. He had been called in from the bush for their regular weekly catch-up with Glenn and the other main players within the program.

'I'll be here or hereabouts. The program covers both southern and East Africa,' Tony assured them. 'You can't get rid of me that easily.'

The three men were sitting in folding canvas camp chairs under a huge mahogany tree in front of Andy's house that sat on a rise, overlooking the sweep of the majestic Zambezi River before them.

The rainy season was now in full swing, but like a giant magnifying glass, the sun had burnt holes in the clouds, with these frequent respites from the rain they knew there would be an uplift in poachers coming across from Zambia. For this reason they were here to plan the season's anti-poaching activities.

'I'd like to keep trying for that male in the corridor,' Tony said, giving name to the area where the most inward and outward poaching insurgence seemed to be centralized.

'Ah, yes, our fugitive valley prince... sure,' Glenn gave his approval. While with the newly formed ZimParks, he and Andy originally found the mutilated bodies of the lone rhino's mother and sibling before Operation Stronghold had even been initiated. 'It may actually dissuade the bastards from using the area.'

Mana Pools was about 180 miles from the corridor, near Tony's bush camp. But instead of traveling across country, the park service had a barge that it used on Lake Kariba for relocation purposes. Tony and his team used this as their mode of transport. It was a straight shot from the nearby township of Kariba up the lake to their camp setup near the Msuna Island Fishing Resort on the Zambezi River. Depending on where they darted the rhinos, they could either relocate them by water or road.

Tony had one of the ranger huts at Mana Pools to use when he was there, not that he used it much. But he enjoyed his time at the park. It gave him a reprieve from the constant grind of anti-poaching and the rigors of camp life.

In the far north of Zimbabwe, Mana Pools was far away from any human settlements that gave the park a distinct feeling of remoteness. It was a pristine wildlife-dense World Heritage site, whose flood plains along the southern shore of the Zambezi turned into a broad expanse of lakes after each rainy season. Mana, meaning "four" in the indigenous Shona language, was in reference to the four large permanent pools formed by the meandering Zambezi. The pools were also home to the country's largest hippo and crocodile population. This thousand square miles, the size of Cape Town on the southern tip of South Africa, was a sprawl of river frontage, islands, sandbanks and pools, flanked by forests of mahogany, wild figs and ebonies. It was one of the least-developed national parks in southern Africa, with only a handful of rangers to patrol its sweeping wilderness.

Being ideal habitat for the black rhinos, but so close to Zambia, the relocation of the park's herd was well underway, saving them but sadly depriving one of the world's wildest and best preserved natural ecological areas of one of its most iconic creatures.

Just as the sun sank behind the hills, painting the peaks gold, Tony walked to the earth-colored, stucco-clad hut set aside for his use. He was distracted, thinking about the lone rhino, the fugitive valley prince, as Glenn called him, but kept a watchful eye on the dusty paths for buffalo and big cats or sunbathing cobras and mambas. Up ahead, a family of warthogs trotted by in military formation. Giraffes glided between the mopanes as languidly as slow-moving summer clouds. From afar, his riverside ranger outpost, hidden among the mahogany trees and white acacias, looked isolated and abandoned, but was as wild as it gets. Bats and doves roosted in the thatch of the huts, lizards zipped across the walls, snakes and scorpions sometimes lurked in dark corners. As he drew closer, he heard the crash of brush, branches snapping, the raining thuds of seedpods. He could see Beauty and his brother Beast with an egret in tow. They were two wild teen bull elephants, camp regulars, who swung by for a snack of seedpods from the sausage trees shading his hut. They stayed close to the ranger's station, seeming to sense it was a place of safety.

Lounging outside its hardwood entrance was his long-time tracker, guide and friend, Ben Mzamo. Ben was of the Matabele tribe, a delicate, bird-boned figure, as angular as a thorn tree, topping five-foot-six in his boot-shod feet, with a tightly cropped head of peppercorn curls and an easy smile. He was incredibly skilled in all manner of bushcraft.

'Ben, you skinny little runt. Where were you last night?' Tony asked, as he strode up to him. They had only returned to the park late last night from Kariba, and Ben had disappeared soon after that. This was the first he'd seen him since then.

'Please, Tony, keep it down. I am not a well man.' Ben was slumped in a chair on the veranda of Tony's hut, with his army-green canvas slouch hat pulled down over his eyes. 'I believe I've been poisoned.'

'Poisoned?' Tony repeated. 'You got pissed last night. You dirty stop-out.'

While out on patrol, he always knew he could rely on Ben, as both their lives depended on their competence. But whenever they came in from the bush, the little man would get into all sorts of scrapes, usually coinciding with rather large women, alcohol and fisticuffs.

Ben lifted the corner of his hat and squinted one blood-shot eye up at him.

'You little bugger.' Tony roughly pulled the hat off his face. Around his eye there was swelling, and beneath it his dark nut-brown complexion had gone a deeper shade of purple. 'And you've been fighting.'

'Ah, it was a thing of beauty. You would've been proud of me.' Ben would be regaling him for days out in the bush with his latest escapade.

'Christ, you had better be good to go. We go back in shortly. A potential scene has been reported up near our camp.' Tony used the Zimbabwean term for a confrontation with poachers.

Ben sat upright, his assumed lethargy forgotten. 'When?' he asked, now deadly serious.

'A couple of minutes ago, the contact was just radioed through.' Tony passed him through the door and grabbed his campaign bag off the bed. 'Ready?' he asked, re-emerging out on the veranda.

'Yes, I'll meet you down at the vehicle,' Ben said over his shoulder, as he rushed into his own hut next door.

'For Christ's sake, stop fidgeting,' Tony said tersely. He was again sitting in the game-viewing hide, later that night on the banks of the Zambezi, with Ben huddled beside him.

The scene they had come to investigate, after their hurried exit from Mana Pools, appeared to be uneventful. One of their team members thought he had seen a line of armed men walking over a ridge line in behind the camp. It had rained before they had got to camp and any sign that was there had been washed away. The only thing in that direction were the holding pens they used to house the captured rhinos, waiting to be relocated.

Tony would usually be alone during these nighttime vigils. He liked the peaceful solitude that these times afforded him. But tonight things were not quite working out that way. Due to Ben's previous night's debouch, as punishment, he had forced the little man to accompany him. Normally, he would be in camp waiting for Tony's radio call, whether to bring in the barge by river or cut a track through the bush for a four-wheel-drive truck to the location of where he had darted the rhino. If he had been successful on the river bank, he intended to send Ben on foot back to camp and bring in the porters to strap down the beast and get it ready for transportation to a protected sanctuary elsewhere in Zimbabwe.

'I need to pee,' Ben said in a small, pensive voice, knowing Tony wouldn't be happy.

'Seriously? You should've sorted that on the way here.' Tony immediately shut him down and concentrated on the peephole in front of him.

They had walked in from their camp several miles downriver. Although 30 long minutes ticked slowly by, without a noise or movement coming from Ben, he could feel the little man's anxious need ratchet up with every passing minute.

'Oh for fuck's sake,' Tony gave in, 'Go, but be quick about it.'

Ben slipped soundlessly out of the hide, but Tony couldn't prevent himself from letting out a long-suffering breath. The little man infuriated him at times, but he knew he could never have a better companion and friend to work with.

He was taken back to when they first met. Tony remembered the moment vividly. They were both on the losing side of the Rhodesian Bush War. Ben was a regular with the Rhodesian African Rifles as a tracker. And even though Tony was born in Botswana, since he had adopted the neighboring country as his home, he would spend six weeks with the Rhodesian Park Service and six weeks with the Rhodesian African Rifles as a field warrant officer. Being an African himself and raised among indigenous tribesmen, Tony never felt more at home among those he considered his equal, black African tribesmen and how they co-existed peacefully with wild animals. With his country of birth predominantly bordering Matabeleland, he naturally gravitated toward the Matabele tribe.

Tony had caught the wildlife bug from his father, an officer with Botswana's Department of Wildlife and National Parks, who raised him alone after his mother died from complications during his birth. An only child, he grew up in 1960s Botswana, when it was wild and free, an untamed Eden, knowing little more than the game parks and the bushveld that had made up his home. His adventurous father, while patrolling the forests and savannas, often took Tony along and taught him to know and love the bush, its animals and the people in it. They lived simply in a spartan riverside ranger's cottage, swam in crocodile-filled rivers and explored the wildest parts of the country. It was high adventure and at times rough and very dangerous. They got stalked by lions, charged by elephants and nearly got washed away in a flash flood. He absorbed everything he saw. By the time he was a teenager, there was no animal or plant he couldn't identify and he kept a meticulous notebook he always carried. Clever and quick-witted, he had a rebellious streak, always talking back. Since his first early homes were a long way from anywhere, Tony was home-schooled and gained no formal qualification. 'Why do you want me to go to university anyway? No more bloody books, please. Animals are my future,' he'd told his somewhat disappointed father, whose footsteps he followed. Instead of beginning his career with Botswana's park service, not wanting to piggy-back on his father's standing, he forged his own path. He moved to neighboring Rhodesia, as Zimbabwe was known before independence, to where as an unknown he could begin to make a name for himself. His headstrong nature and fearlessness helped him carve out a Tarzan-like reputation as a young man dedicated to wildlife conservation throughout southern Africa.

Tony first laid eyes on Ben while on patrol when the little man had been seconded to his unit. While Tony was a good tracker and used this skill constantly with the park service, Ben took it to another level, with him it was a gift. On patrol inside Wankie National Park, as Hwange was known under white Rhodesian rule, just south of the Matetsi River, they had come across a well-worn pathway of many shod footprints. In the park this could only mean man. Since this was a protected wildlife enclave, this meant these footprints were out of place and heading inland toward the still-active tourist destination of Victoria Falls.

Tony went down on his haunches beside Ben, who was intently studying the sign. He'd been watching the little man for most of the day and realized he was good, but didn't appreciate how good until he asked for his opinion. 'Well?' he asked in Sindebele. Animal tracks were one thing, but those of man hadn't registered large with his skillset until he had become embroiled in this bush war and spent a lot of his enlisted time out on patrol.

Ben was silent for perhaps another minute before he spoke. 'Twenty-five. Mostly new recruits, being used as pack mules. Ten are male, five are female. But there are ten seasoned ZIPRA terrs, guerrillas, as well. The recruits are carrying the armaments for the veterans. They are going after the soft target at Victoria Falls.'

Tony rocked back on his heels. *Good lord, all that from what looked like a dusty confusion of overlaid footprints*, he thought but decided against voicing his opinion. 'Are you sure?' he asked, but more to give himself time to think than as a question of the little man's skill.

Ben only raised a scornful eyebrow. He didn't deem to reply.

Tony knew he had to call in a stop line between here and the falls. This group had to be stopped before it reached the tourist destination. 'How old is the spoor?' he asked, now fully accepting Ben's assessment.

'One hour, two at the most,' the Matabele answered decisively.

Tony pulled a map out of a waterproof pouch in his webbing. Looking at it, he calculated time and distance.

Ben lent over and laid his finger on the map. 'They will need to cross the Matetsi River. They will do it here. They will stay in the park until they have skirted the Kazuma Pan. They will then either try for the airport or go for the township itself.' He smiled and added wryly, 'Of course, this is only my humble opinion.'

'Of course,' Tony repeated sarcastically, but already liking this intelligent, articulate little man. Tracking animals was one thing, but man? This was a very different sort of beast. Reluctantly, he deferred back to the diminutive tracker, so far what he had said made sense. 'And in your humble opinion,' he said tongue-in-cheek, 'where would you set up the stop line?'

After a moment, Ben stabbed a finger at the map. 'That hill, to the south of the airport. Our troops can be choppered in, the other side of the service hangers. Their arrival won't attract too much attention. The hill is less than two miles from there. They can be on site in less than 15 minutes. We will have the true run of spoor by then, and can relay it to the stop line.'

Tony liked what he had heard. He called up his radio operator and radioed through the coordinates. The stop-line troop would be choppered in from Bulawayo, and on site in approximately two hours.

'How far ahead are they?' Tony asked Ben. It was 20 miles to the airport.

'Five miles, ten at the most.' Ben stooped and scanned the spoor. 'But they are heavily burdened, and moving slowly.' He made another calculation. 'If we run, we will be directly behind them when they hit the stop line.'

Tony quickly hatched a plan, but before voicing it he realized he didn't even know the name of the man he was putting so much faith in. He looked at the tracker and asked in Sindebele, 'How are you called?' He liked this Matabele, he obviously had an independent spirit, was decisive and unafraid to give his opinion, even if it wasn't asked for.

'Ben… Ben Mzamo.' He had been commanded by many of these white men before, but this one was different. There was no assumed attitude of superiority. He had a good feeling about him, he was a man he could give his respect to.

'Well, Ben Mzamo, you are obviously a man with a plan,' Tony said, converting Ben's last name to its literal meaning, 'Take the spoor.'

They soon developed a formidable partnership that started in one brutal bush war and progressed into another.

They ran on the spoor in the inverted V. Ben was at the center and Tony and his corporal were running on opposite flanks protecting him. The other two men of the stick brought up the rear. The three men at the front used a series of whistles, bird calls and hand signals, when they were in sight, to direct the run of spoor.

Within the first hour, Tony knew they were rapidly overhauling the insurgents, and within another hour they would virtually be on top of them. He could see Ben had unerringly predicted the line that they were taking. They appeared to be trying for the airport.

Five miles out, Tony called his first stop of the hot pursuit. He didn't want to spring the trap prematurely and have the insurgents bombshell, running off in 25 different directions. He needed what he planned to work as a classic ambush and counter-ambush. Once the enemy ran onto the stop line it was his intention for his stick to catch them in a pincer movement, cutting off any escape.

Tony called up his radioman. The stop line was in position, but they hadn't seen anything yet. He squatted down beside Ben, who was again studying the spoor. 'How far ahead are they?'

'Less than two miles. I would've called a stop if you didn't. They would've heard us if we ran for much longer. They had started leapfrogging.'

'Meaning?' Tony asked, as he looked around, trying to determine where to place his men to catch the insurgents if they retreated.

Ben noticed his field officer's assessment of their surroundings and didn't begrudge him the question. 'They have been leaving men on their back-trail, guarding their rear the closer they get to their target.' He then voiced his one main concern. 'I think whoever is leading this group is a veteran of many missions. We will have trouble with him today.'

Tony had picked up the apprehension in the tracker's voice. 'And you say this, why?'

'The way he has his men under control. Even though most of the group are heavily burdened, he has kept them in order, allowing none to lag behind. And he is also using his soldiers, the real men in the group, in front, behind and out on both flanks. He is very wary.'

'And you read all this while we were running?' Tony asked, impressed with his extraordinary skill.

'I have been doing this since the start of the war, following the spoor of men.' He shrugged his shoulders. 'I am still alive, and would like to keep it that way.'

'Makes two of us. Okay, I may not know bush war like you, but I know animals, and when they are trapped, they panic. Most will run, but some will stand and fight. This leader you talk of, he will be one of the latter.' Tony looked around again and then at Ben. 'If you were him, what would you do when your men run onto the stop line?'

Ben liked Tony all the more for asking the question, most field officers wouldn't have thought it this far through. 'He will sacrifice the new recruits… leave them to their fate,' he said after thinking about it. 'He will gather his seasoned soldiers and then set up a fighting retreat. Initially, directly away from the stop line. But he will already have planned his escape.'

'That all makes sense.'

'Can I see the map?' Ben studied it for less than a minute, looked at the angle of the sun, then gave his opinion. 'He will run for the river, in this direction,' he pointed to the map. 'He or one of the men with him know the key through the security cordon. He will have his soldiers run a rearguard action, effectively a tactical withdrawal.' He stabbed at the map. 'He will run down this valley and try to get through the minefield along this stretch of the river.'

In an attempt to prevent insurgents coming in from across the Zambezi River, the Rhodesian Security Forces had laid down a 100-mile minefield on their side of the river, with a density of 9,000 mines per mile. But as with every well-laid security cordon like this one, there was a key. It was a closely guarded secret kept by the Rhodesian Police Armaments, but like everything that was set into a given pattern, once the key was known a pathway through the minefield could be established.

Tony didn't like the odds. He had five in his stick and, if what Ben said was true, there could be ten seasoned insurgents. 'Okay, we need to get to this valley. Can you initially get us parallel to it, down to this narrow gut?' He pointed to a side canyon that intersected the valley that Ben believed the terrs would use to make their escape.

'Of course.' Ben realized Tony wanted to avoid the escape valley itself so as not to leave any tracks and warn the insurgents of their presence.

'Good.' Tony called his men to him and explained his plan. 'Once we make the valley, we will set up here and here,' he showed them on his map where he would lay their own stop line, and hopefully stop the insurgents retreat. He looked at his watch, calculating time and distance again. He knew from experience there was an Air Rhodesian afternoon flight due to take off shortly from the Vic Falls Airport. They had an hour.

He looked at Ben for confirmation. The little man nodded in agreement.

'Okay, go,' Tony ordered. 'Get us there.'

Jacob Vusa hadn't liked this mission, not when it had been first outlined to him, not now, or at any time leading up to this moment. Tall, tough and ruggedly handsome, he was a heartless bandit. Born of proud Matabele blood, he grew up poor on the mean streets on the outskirts of Bulawayo. He was a broad-shouldered but finely muscled man, gained from years of insurgency and living roughly in the bush. His animal cunning had helped him survive the brutal years of the Rhodesian Bush War.

He knew the area they were in and had travelled it many times since he had become a freedom fighter. The only profession he'd ever known. Taken as a stripling youth by a persuasive recruitment officer, he had become Soviet trained and indoctrinated, as were most of the Matabele ZIPRA insurgent fighters involved in the Rhodesian conflict, and turned into a machine used for nothing more than killing. He had been fighting in this bush war since its inception, thrown in at the deep end and survived unscathed. He had risen through the ranks and become a commander within ZIPRA, the military wing of the Marxist-Leninist political party ZANU. His murderous efficiency caught the attention of the Rhodesian Intelligence and he became a man with a price on his head.

Vusa didn't like being around new recruits. He worked better alone. They were clumsy and dangerous, but courtesy of the discipline instilled by his Soviet instructors, he would follow orders, until the danger became too great for him to follow them any longer. Despite his communist indoctrination, he had an independent spirit that had made him an unpredictable yet successful weapon.

The plan for this mission was to try for one of the civilian Air Rhodesia's Viscount airplanes, during it ascent from the Victoria Falls Airport. It was a shock-and-awe mission, designed by Soviet intelligence, attempting to dishearten the white minority Rhodesian government and bring them to the bargaining table.

Five new recruits each carried a SA-7, a light-weight, shoulder-fired, surface-to-air missile system, designed to target aircraft during low-altitude flight. The SAM had a passive infrared homing-guidance system, complete with a high-explosive warhead. The other recruits carried two warheads for each system, with two seasoned veterans overseeing each group. This was the first time a mission of this audacious caliber had been tried, and Vusa had been told if this was successful, the eventual spoils of war available to him would be incalculable. He didn't believe these sentiments for a minute. He lived for the atrocities of war, the maiming and the killing, and for the moment that was enough for him.

Once they reached the hill overlooking the airport, Vusa would set up a semi-circular ring of launchers to take out the fat and lumbering target. He had chosen the best of his veterans to service the launchers, they had all been trained with the system. Once he had seen the aircraft hit the ground, he wouldn't be sticking around. He knew the wrath of the Rhodesian Security Forces, who would chase him to and across the border. He wanted to be through the minefield, and over the river, well inside Zambia by nightfall. He had an hour to set up and then run for the border. The new recruits could keep up or not. He really didn't care.

Even with the other veterans, Vusa still didn't like it. The group was unwieldy and left a trail a blind man could follow. But as yet nothing had shown up on his back-trail. He looked at the cheap digital watch he wore.

He would set up in half an hour. If anything, the hated white government's rigorously tight airline schedule would be their undoing. He looked around disgustedly at the new recruits who had slumped down exhausted after their long trek. Cannon fodder was all he saw. Then his eyes settled on one of the female recruits. She lowered her eyes, trying not to attract his attention. He had used this girl the night before they had crossed the river. She had been the comeliest of them all. She struggled, not like the others who had just lay there whimpering like beaten puppies. She had been the best of the female recruits to pick from since leaving the Zambian capital of Lusaka four days previously. He looked at his watch again. *No, he didn't have time*. Once he was across the river, and if she was still with them, he would take her again tonight. His lust and the carnage he was about to inflict would only heighten his pleasure. He repositioned himself, it was time to get the launch teams into position.

Vusa looked up at the hill he had chosen to site his team upon. Even though he couldn't see the airport, he knew it would give him an open field of fire on the other side. He scoured over the maps his Soviet instructors had given him and had the lay of the land fixed in his mind. He would make any necessary adjustments once they had gained the crest of the hill. He would take the center and direct his teams on to the target from there. If the plane was successfully targeted within the first few launches, he might be able to try for the airport itself. That would certainly be a bonus.

The only issue was the open clearing of ground they had to traverse before the hill's ascent. He was standing beneath the overhang sweep of a large African ebony tree, using the binoculars, the only item other than his AK-47 that he carried on missions. Nothing looked out of place, but the clearing would mean he and his troops would be exposed before getting to the base of the hill. He had no choice and had to get the launch teams into position before running out of time. Bringing up all his section heads, he pointed out where he wanted each of their teams to go. He watched as they led their recruits out on to the clearing. When all five teams were committed he followed.

Vusa was halfway across the clearing when, literally, firstly the far-left team, then the right dissolved before his eyes. 'Shit… shit!' he swore.

They had been made, walking onto a cunningly set up stop line. He pivoted on the spot, and rushed back into the trees. Once he was under cover, he looked back out on to the open plain. 'Damn it!' The three central teams had also been shafted with heavy machine-gun fire. He didn't bother returning fire to avoid drawing attention to himself. Most of his team had been wiped out. He only counted three of his seasoned veterans making the tree line again. None of the new recruits had made it. They were either dead or too shell-shocked to know what to do. He gathered the remaining veterans around him. Without looking back, he ran with his men towards the border.

What an absolute trouncing, he thought bitterly. He would like to meet the man who set up this artfully executed ambush. He put the thought aside as he ran, not expecting that he would ever get his wish.

Tony had got his stick through the gut, and set up his stop line where Ben had indicated in the perpendicular valley. He was positioning his machine gunner when he picked up the rattling susurration of distant automatic fire.

'Goddamn it,' he swore. That was a close-run thing, he had only just got the men into position in time. He glanced over at Ben, who had a cheeky I-told-you-so smile splashed across his face. 'Bloodthirsty little bugger.'

The little man seemed to be reveling with anticipation at the impending action.

'Christ,' Tony mumbled, 'give me a gut-shot lion any day rather than this.' He knew he would never get used to this senseless war. He checked his FN FAL semi-automatic, and that the magazines were easily accessible in his webbing. He and his men were about ten miles from the contact, with another ten miles behind him to the border. He calculated, if there were any insurgents left, they would be here in an hour, running headlong for the border. It was now time to wait.

Losing patience, Tony felt like it was the slowest hour of his life. 'The bloody thing must have stopped.' He gave his stainless-steel Rolex a shake, holding it up to his ear. 'No, still working,' he realized, as he looked down at the second-hand crawling around the dial. He looked over at Ben. Like a Cheshire cat, the little shit still had that grin of anticipation on his face.

Ben seemed to sense Tony's look and returned his gaze.

If it was going to come, it would be any minute now, both men knew. Tony just hoped the little Matabele was wrong and the insurgents hadn't chosen this valley for their escape.

Tony wasn't ready for it when the shooting started. Ben had anticipated which side of the valley the insurgents would use. His machine gunner had opened up an instant after Ben's initial raking hail of bullets. Tony saw two men hit before the group of men dove for cover. Just like that it was over before he realized it, and he hadn't even fired a shot.

'Damn it!' Vusa fumed, they had run headlong into another ambush. Two more of his men had gone down, but he kept moving. He couldn't afford to be pinned down, not here, not this close to the border. As he rolled over, looking for cover, he realized all the fire had come from his right, with nothing from the left. He attracted the attention of his last remaining man, indicating to cover him as he got set to run. He could care less about the man. When the man was firing, he sprinted. He had drawn all of the fire, getting shafted with bullets from multiple positions, and was as good as dead. He was up and running again, jinxing to the left. He was nearly through the line; all its fire was directed to the right.

'Oh shit,' Vusa swore, right in front of him there was a big white man leveling a rifle, about to bring it to bear. He kept running, he had to reach the border.

Tony saw his men open up again. They were firing at one of the insurgents off to his left, but he realized too late it was a diversion. Someone, a tall menacing-looking black man, was running directly towards him. Too late, he started to sight his FN. Before he knew it, the man was on top of him, smashing his rifle away, it fell to the ground. A knee caught him in his chest, driving the wind from his lungs. He was thrown over backwards, but not before he grabbed the man's scruffy Bata Bullet-clad foot. They tumbled down in a heap together, both wrestling for ascendancy. Tony copped another knee, this time to his face, as the man tried to club him down with the butt of his AK-47. He grabbed for the rifle and tried to yank it from his hands. Before the man released the gun, he was swinging a roundhouse punch to his head. Tony shrugged and hunched his shoulder. The fist bounced off the rubbery muscles of his upper arm and flew up over his head.

'Not so quickly,' he said in Sindebele, and drove his own fist up into the big black man's face.

'*Impungushe*, jackal,' Vusa growled in the same language. He had to quickly get passed this white man or his *izinja*, his dogs, would soon be on to him. He kneed, gnashed his teeth and punched. He fought as if his life depended on it as it surely did. If the Rhodesians caught him, he was as good as dead. He had perpetrated far too many atrocities for them to go unpunished. He kneed again, but this white man just wouldn't give up. He took the binoculars from around his head and using the strap, swung with all his might. It caught his adversary on the point of his jaw, just below his ear. The man slumped, Vusa dropped the glasses, tripped and stumbled slightly over the white man, and was running again. He had to get to the minefield before it was too dark to establish the key. He hoped he would never meet this cursed white bastard again.

Tony slowly came to. Ben was squatting beside him, ghoulishly staring at the lump on the side of his head, clucking at the patchwork of injuries he had sustained. 'What happened?' he asked.

He noticed the other members of his stick were also morbidly looking on.

'You let him get away,' was all Ben said.

'What? Who?' Tony was getting back his wits and then he remembered.

'The leader. He's still running for the border.'

'Well, don't just talk about it, go.' Tony wanted another crack at the big Matabele.

They had been running for an hour. It was just on dusk and Tony knew they were near the river. 'Why are we stopping?' he asked. He had only just thrown off his lethargy and made his way to the front of the column again.

'We are at the security cordon. The man we have been chasing has gone in there,' Ben pointed with his chin, past the single strand of high-tensile wire, hung with small metal disks, depicting a skull-and-crossbones danger warning.

'But I thought he would need someone who knew the key?' Tony had hoped this was where they would catch the insurgent leader.

Ben didn't answer. It was obvious the man they were chasing knew the key himself, and there was nothing or nobody who would make him go in there. 'Damn it,' he heard Tony curse, coming to the same realization.

Tony was smarting at allowing the man to get away. He would never forget that face and only hoped they would cross paths with this thug again.

But hidden beneath the leafy foliage of the riverine bush, Vusa was thinking very similar thoughts. He knew somehow he would meet this white bastard again. He just didn't realize it would be during a different kind of war, one fought not for land, but instead for an elusive breed of prehistoric beast that roamed among it.

CHAPTER 3

Tony and Ben Discover the Poachers Mode of Transport

ONCE BEN CRAWLED out of the game hide, the sky turned dark, thunder lit the clouds and the heavens opened up. A ferocious rainstorm kicked up. Watching the ragged flashes of lightning and the seasonal rain pelting down, Tony was thankful he was under the cover of the canvas screen. He didn't envy Ben and his ill-timed need to relieve himself. 'Stupid bugger,' he berated him, 'deserves it.' He peered out through the peephole and couldn't see a thing, except for the deluge of water. When Ben finally made his way back after the downpour passed, Tony decided *I'll make the little bastard wait outside while he dries off*. He didn't want him increasing the humidity of the already stuffy conditions inside the hide. Then he heard a sound that didn't fit in with the rain and his surroundings. He still couldn't see a thing, but was sure he'd heard what sounded like a motor. 'Surely not,' he murmured, 'not this far up the river.' He was tempted to go out into the rain, but thought better of it. It was dry and relatively comfortable in the hide. He would wait until Ben was back and he'd send him out again since he'd already be wet. He allowed himself to be lulled by the persistent rain.

Miraculously, a little while later, Ben appeared out of the darkness, crawling back into the hide. 'Big trouble, Tony,' were the first words out of his mouth as he dragged a sopping hand over his water-drenched face.

'Whaddya mean?' Tony stared at him, confused. He'd been away for perhaps ten or 15 minutes at most.

'We've got poachers. They just came out of the bush and were taken off the beach in front of us.'

'How?' He hadn't heard or seen a thing. Then he remembered hearing what he thought was a motor.

'Pontoon boat. Looked like one of any number found up and down the lake. I'd walked off the track and was sheltering under a jackalberry waiting for the rain to stop, and they literally walked right past me, down to the river,' he indicated in front of them. 'I followed them, and there was the boat waiting. Bow first, nosed up onto the beach.'

'How many?' Tony was perplexed by this sudden revelation, but knew Ben would have taken note of their number.

'I counted 20, excluding the one who brought in the boat. A big group.'

'Are you sure they were poachers?'

'Tony, who else would they have been?' Ben didn't wait for an answer. 'Plus, five of them were carrying AKs, and one looked like he had a big .375 Magnum. But I couldn't be sure.' He was silent for a moment as he thought about what he'd seen. 'I think most of them were porters. Four or five men per rifle, as they were carrying heavy bundles.'

'Oh shit! But where had they come from?' Tony asked with foreboding, but more a question to himself than Ben. He made a decision, the rhino they were after put aside for now. 'We'll have to wait until it's light and try and backtrack them.' If anyone could do it after a deluge like that, Tony knew Ben would be able to.

'Sure,' Ben agreed, 'but don't hold your breath. That was a helluva downpour, and the reason they come in during the rainy season, so their spoor is washed away.'

The dawn's early light couldn't come fast enough for Tony. They searched the beach below the hide but found nothing, and he had Ben on the back-trail before it was fully light.

Initially, the little man had trouble following the incoming spoor, but eventually as the sunlight strengthened he followed it more easily. At times Tony couldn't see any sign at all and it seemed Ben followed it by instinct alone, but at other times the trail was clear for him to see.

A couple of hours before noon and Tony knew exactly where they were going. Seeing white-backed vultures circling on the crest of the forested hill, he was full of dread. 'Yeah, poachers,' he spat disgustedly.

The poachers had hit them and hit them hard, wiping out all the rhinos they had tranquilized for hundreds of miles around. They had hit Stronghold's holding stockade, up in the hills behind Tony's camp at the Msuna Fishing Resort.

When they arrived to the macabre scene, Tony was so horrified he only uttered one word: 'Wow!' The sheer brutality and scale of this took his breath away as he stood looking over the dead animals they had so painstakingly tracked, darted and brought to this location for later transportation to far more secure sanctuaries elsewhere in Zimbabwe. Twenty-five adults and seven calves had been slaughtered, with half their faces bludgeoned off, so their valuable horns could be removed. And the 15 bullet-riddled rangers guarding the stockade had been murdered. They had been surrounded and ambushed, wiped out to the man.

On the chaotic morning of the atrocity, Tony, angry and disgusted, immediately called up the transportation barge. He knew it was a long shot, but he was going to board any pontoon boat in the vicinity. He had already called through the attack to Glenn Tatum and Andy Woodward and had been given approval to search all vessels on Lake Kariba. Andy would be doing the same from the head of the dam, from Kariba township itself. The police were on their way, but it would be hours before they would be on site. Tony wasn't prepared to sit around, he needed to take some sort of action.

'Hey Tony,' Ben called, following him down to where the barge was moored. 'We need to think this through.'

'Not for something like this we don't. We're gonna search every fucking pontoon boat on the goddamn lake.'

Resigned to what would follow, Ben trailed him as he stepped onto the barge.

Tony behaved like his heart was on fire. Because it was.

All he could think about was the bloodied, mutilated bodies of all the rhinos and rangers. And the little calves, lying beside their mothers, with half of their faces, ripped off, frozen in agony. Only the day before they were as frisky and playful as puppies. He felt like he was fighting his worst nightmare, even though he prepared for it his entire life, he'd never seen anything so chilling.

Tony and Ben had just spent a fruitless day, boarding and searching every boat they came across on the lake. They talked sparingly. Tony was uncharacteristically quiet. For most of the day he sat in hunched-shouldered silence, his eyes angrily sweeping the lake. Every time he saw a boat he went into a frenzy. The loss he felt was overwhelming and spilled over to rage. Ben had already had to step in and prevent him from assaulting two men who were clearly British tourists, as well as an abrasive ex-pat Afrikaner out for a spot of leisurely fishing. It was obvious none of them were poachers, but Tony didn't care. All he was looking to do was vent his simmering rage.

Just as the evening light dimmed, Tony had begun to settle down somewhat. They were about two hours north of the jetty at Msuna, when Ben spotted a large expensive-looking pontoon boat. It was turning after reversing out from being nose-in on the Zambian side of the lake. How they had missed it earlier in the day, he didn't have a clue.

'Tony,' he said, 'look up ahead on the far-right bank.'

Tony appeared to be mollified, but he had taken the hit personally, racked with guilt for not being able to protect the rhinos. He had spent months collecting those animals, not to mention the loss of the rangers, whom he considered to be friends, family even.

'Speed up and bring us alongside,' he called to the barge captain, who was in awe of Tony's temper after the afternoon's performance. His strops were a glorious sight to behold.

Ben shot a look at the captain who laughed nervously. They both knew a storm was coming.

Inching closer, Tony motioned furiously for the pontoon boat to stop. When it didn't, he instructed the captain to ram the boat, causing it to rock dramatically.

'Easy,' a big black man shouted out in Sindebele, as he stepped up from the cabin below. He bent over, inspecting the side of the barge. 'You'll be responsible for any damages.'

'The fuck we will,' Tony shouted back, confronting the man as he easily jumped from the barge onto the boat.

Ben groaned, 'Here we go again.' Knowing how hot-headed and explosive Tony could be, he rushed after him to de-escalate the situation.

As soon as Tony stepped foot on the boat and stood in front of the muscular, mean-faced black man, he swore he had met him somewhere before. Before he could think about it further, Ben was standing beside him. 'Park service business, there are poachers in the area, we need to search your vessel.'

'I don't think so,' the man said in a very clear and firm voice in Sindebele. He was supremely confident and not the sort of person who could be easily intimidated.

'You can think what you like, pal.' Tony took a step forward to within inches of his face. Their eyes were level. 'By government decree, I have the right to search and seize, as well as shoot poachers on site.' Without taking his eyes off the big man, he spoke to Ben who stood beside him. 'Search it.'

The guy glared at him, his chest heaving, disdain pouring out of him.

Ben hesitated, his eyes flicked nervously toward him. He didn't like this standoff, but there wasn't a lot he could do about it.

The man would have tried to prevent Ben, if Tony hadn't warned him again.

'You just fucking try.' Tony took another step forward, forcing the man backwards. 'I lost good men today and I won't hesitate to have your boat confiscated, taken to Kariba and pulled apart, piece by fucking piece.'

'As you wish,' the man acceded grudgingly, 'but you are going to hear about this transgression.'

They watched each other warily while Ben searched the boat. After several minutes of searching, he brought a big .375 Holland & Holland Magnum up from down below. He gave it to Tony who in turn shot the bolt and put his nose to the breech. Ben spoke briefly to him, out of earshot of the man.

'Why has this rifle been recently fired?' Tony questioned. 'And why do you have blood on the deck at the bow and in the cabin?'

'Crocodiles. We had to shoot them after they began taking our bait.'

'We? You and who else? There's nobody else onboard.'

'I have already dropped them off, on the Zambia side,' he answered tersely. He had no excuse why there was blood below deck. 'I have committed no crime.'

'We'll see about that.' Tony knew he was lying and sensed he was in the presence of a sophisticated wildlife smuggler, likely abetted by a cadre of corrupt officials.

'You are wasting my time… you have no proof of any kind.'

He knew this man was guilty of something, he just wasn't sure what yet. 'Consider yourself under arrest.' He turned to Ben. 'Fend off the barge and get us underway to Kariba.'

'Campbell, you are going to regret this.'

This raised Tony's suspicions. 'How do you know my name?' He knew from the get-go that there was something familiar about the man.

'I always make a note of knowing who among us are the vanquished,' he said spitefully. 'You lost against me once before, and this time will be no different.' He nonchalantly sat down on the padded bench seat behind him, and looked out over the side.

Tony suddenly realized he was the terrorist leader who had escaped from him years ago. He racked his brain. Rhodesian Intelligence had run a full investigation after Tony has set up the ambush. They had taken and analyzed the leader's discarded AK-47. From fingerprints and ballistic testing determined it had been involved in multiple insurgent actions and that it belonged to Jacob Vusa, ZIPRA officer and a key member of the Matabele political wing's armed insurgents.

'You are out of favor now, Vusa,' Tony taunted the big Matabele. 'We'll see who's truly the vanquished. I know you're a fucking criminal and I'm not done with you yet.'

A .375 Holland & Holland Magnum and blood on the bow and in the cabin of this pontoon boat was no proof of his involvement, but Tony's keen instinct warned him the guy was somehow involved in last night's poaching raid. He would have the boat confiscated and let the police forensics pull it apart.

The day after the raid, when the Vusa saga had played itself out at the police station, Tony was back at the Mana Pools ranger station arguing with Glenn. He looked drained, unshaven and with five o'clock shadows under his eyes like he hadn't slept and had clearly been badly affected by the killings.

'The guy's as guilty as sin,' he huffed in frustration. 'And you know it.'

'Tony, you know a recently shot rifle and some indeterminable blood isn't proof.'

'And the bullshit lie about crocodiles taking his fishing bait, ridiculous. Never heard of crocodiles attacking boats. There wasn't a scrap of fishing equipment anywhere.'

'I'm sure you're right, but we don't have enough evidence.' Glenn tried to placate him. 'Plus the bastard may have backed the wrong horse during the war, but he still has connections within the new government.'

'Oh for fuck's sake, didn't we all.' Tony simmered with fury. 'So we're just letting the bastard go?'

'No choice. The matter is closed.' Glenn collapsed in the chair behind his desk with an exasperated sigh. 'He's just been released.'

'Fucking unbelievable… corrupt motherfucker. I should've shot him when I had the chance.'

'Get over it, Tony.'

'I know it's bloody well him.' Knowing this obvious poacher was getting away with a massacre only inflamed his sense of injustice. 'This isn't over yet,' he shouted over his shoulder as he stalked off.

Glenn had grown used to his surly outbursts. But he was troubled by Vusa's sudden release too. Tony may have been as wild and willful as a leopard, but he also knew he was rarely wrong about anything. There was a sense that this mass killing would lead to other massacres and they had to be hyper-vigilant.

The white-minority government of Rhodesia was eventually forced by international pressure to give up power and work towards an amicable independence in 1980, nearly two decades after most other countries on the continent. And people like Jacob Vusa, who were trained and backed by the Soviets, were treated no better than outcasts after independence. They were predominantly from the Matabele tribe, with their ZANU political leaders defeated by an overwhelming popular vote from the rival Chinese-backed Shona tribe. Tribalism had reared its ugly head.

With the end of white rule and the buffer gone between the country's two main tribes, the previous centuries-old subjugation the Matabele had forced upon the Shona people before British colonialism was now turned full-force back on them. Jacob Vusa was thanked for his role in winning the new Zimbabwe, but there were no spoils of war or booty for him to claim. Unable to even retain a place in the new Zimbabwean Army, he was treated as a pariah and forced into a different type of oppression. He and his military prowess were snubbed, since he had lost the country he had so recently helped to claim. Vusa may have won his freedom from beneath the yoke of white rule, but little else. All he knew was years of fighting, with only the land he had ravaged now firmly imprinted on his mind. It soon became apparent, a new war was open to him, with trained insurgents to command, but this time a war he could profit from.

After independence, having lived for so long in Lusaka during the bush war, his skills didn't go unnoticed by the still-resident Soviets. With the Soviet Embassy in Lusaka being the largest in southern Africa, Vusa found himself one of the Soviet's 500 military personnel based in the neighboring capital, ostensibly there to assist training the Zambian Defense Force. Being involved with the importation and transportation of over half-a-billion-dollars' worth of arms to be used, in theory, by the Zambians, it didn't take Vusa long to become involved with the reciprocal trade of contraband. While it wasn't the Soviets that introduced Vusa to the world of banned wildlife trade, they helped him establish the smuggling route up into the *entrepôt* of Burundi, at the top of Lake Tanganyika, sandwiched between the Democratic Republic of the Congo to the west and Tanzania to the east.

With the Soviet's support and funneling of arms in from Zambia, a Tutsi colonel in the Burundi Army led a bloodless coup and took over the small landlocked African country. The colonel drafted a new constitution and set up a one-party state. Vusa, with his Soviet military instruction and as equally important, a black face, became instrumental in assisting the new Burundi governing regime with their suppression of any political opponents.

It was during this time that he cemented his relationships with the ruling

Tutsi tribe and established his pipeline for wildlife contraband. Desperate for hard currency, the new Burundi officialdom first assisted and then openly supported Vusa's supply and importation of these illicit goods. The plundered goods that his previously unemployed brothers-in-arms reaped from the land weren't smuggled, but openly transported as diplomatic trade goods. From Lusaka, the contraband was driven up the Zambian M2, through to the harbor township of Mpulungu, on the southern tip of Lake Tanganyika, and ferried by Burundi's government barge to the top end of the lake, to the country's economic capital, Bujumbura. Courtesy of newly-established silent partners in the Tutsi government, importation duties were waived and a bonded warehouse was made available to him. The goods were held for transshipment there, depending on their type, for either Taiwan or the Middle East.

Severing his ties with the Soviets, he established himself as the kingpin in the southern African rhino-horn trade by helping to feed the brisk demand for exotic creatures in southeast Asia. He dabbled in ivory, but his main focus fell squarely on the harvesting, transportation and sales of rhino horn. He was supplying over 70 percent of the southern African horn via his collection base in Lusaka and transshipment depot in Burundi.

By the mid-1980s, his wildlife-smuggling racket expanded beyond his wildest imagining and he accumulated prime real estate in the newly independent Zimbabwe as well as in Zambia. But it was the discovery of oil in the second-largest sovereign state on the southern tip of the Arabian Peninsula, Yemen, that contributed substantially to Vusa's newfound wealth and freedom. Initially concentrating on powdered horn being shipped to Taiwan for its supposed "medicinal" benefits at many thousands of dollars per pound, supplied as a substitute for the far rarer Asian rhino horn, it took one brief meeting for this to only account for a fraction of his overall sales.

A Zanzibar Arab, whom he dealt with initially in ivory, asked a seemingly innocuous question concerning rhino horn. He wanted to know if he could purchase raw horn for the construction of the much-coveted Arabian *jambiya*. One of Vusa's talents was to sniff out a profit and see potential were others didn't. It didn't take him long to learn the rhino-horn handle dagger was lusted over as the proudest mark of manhood within the Yemenis state. With overflowing Yemenis coffers flush with the proceeds from crude oil, even an ordinary Yemeni was able to buy one of these prized blades. He cut out the middleman and began manufacturing the *jambiya* in his warehouse complex in Lusaka. He soon had more money than he knew what to do with.

By now Vusa had become the most monstrously prolific poacher in southern Africa. While he sourced rhino horn from all over the continent, his most profitable source was found in his own adopted backyard. In a few short years, due to the fall in copper prices and the disastrous economic conditions in Zambia, he led a group of now-outcast Matabele insurgents in the plundering of one rich Zambian wilderness area after another. He decimated each pristine sanctuary of wildlife into a ravaged wasteland. He and his group contributed in the massacre of 4,000 black rhino, along with a vast percentage of some 50,000 elephants throughout Zambia. Vusa brought in a massive haul of ivory and over 20,000 pounds of valuable horn and contributed to one of the largest travesties and devastation of a rare and irreplaceable treasure.

As the Zambian wildlife resource began to dry up, his predatory eyes fell further south, to his home country, Zimbabwe. But herein lay a previously nonexistent problem. Zimbabwe's economy was still intact, with a resourcefully aggressive wildlife management service, headed by tenaciously combative conservationists, like his one-time adversary, Tony Campbell.

Vusa had known of Campbell's reputation for a few years, as he slowly had his Matabele poachers infiltrate Zimbabwe's national parks and began supplying him with the rich plunder from across the Zambezi. But Campbell was the last person he expected to board his boat the previous night, and it wasn't until then that he realized exactly who he was, remembering him after their wartime skirmish. Instinctively knowing it had been Campbell's planning that had nearly been his undoing years ago, when he had to fight for his life to escape the artful trap he had set.

He wouldn't underestimate him again, knowing Campbell was as tenacious as a crocodile and wouldn't stop hunting him. But his intelligence had told him the white man had left Operation Stronghold, and taken up a position with the WWF. The raid would have been planned very differently had he known he was still in the vicinity. It had been a disconcertingly close-run thing. He was well aware how single-minded and relentless Campbell had become, with many of his poachers being killed or captured by him, ever since he had established himself and run his burgeoning poaching enterprise from Lusaka. But with this raid, he had taken personal charge and for the first time in many years put feet on the ground in an area he had grown to know so intimately during his wartime forays. He wanted first-hand knowledge of how best to loot this country's last great resource, before closing up shop and venturing off to a life of retired luxury, floating around on a boat and finally seeing the world.

He had only just unloaded the horn, seen the motley crew of Matabele poachers and Zambian porters to the waiting trucks, and got back on board before Campbell had seized his boat. Still it had been a stunningly swift raid, considering the bountiful haul he'd reaped, over 300-pounds of horn. But it had cost him dearly to have that white dog Campbell called off and his vessel returned to him.

Yes, it had been a very close-run thing, he reflected. Campbell would definitely bear watching. But the raid had served its purpose, and now he needed to get back to Lusaka to process the horn and plan his next poaching expedition.

CHAPTER 4

Operation Crash

TONY WAS THOUGHTFUL but had a temper, which he brilliantly put to use when he needed to slash through the wildlife service's tangled mess of rules and red tape. After being curtly dismissed by Glenn Tatum, he followed his hunch and headed up the lake in the parks service barge, to the location where they had originally seized Vusa's pontoon boat. Nosing into the shore, Tony had the captain drop off him and Ben and instructed him to return later that afternoon when they radioed for a pick-up.

'Yes,' Ben affirmed as they stepped on shore, 'I count about 20 prints. A large force, all dropped off by boat from the lake. It appears some were heavily burdened.'

Tony had calmed down since the meeting with Glenn and was thinking clearly.

'Okay, so this is where he dropped off the poachers after they were picked up in front of the hide.' There was no doubt for Tony that "he" was Vusa. In his mind, the guy was the kingpin and guilty as sin, just as he had tried to convince his boss. 'We should find vehicle tracks further up the bank.'

Within 200 yards of the lake shore Tony and Ben came upon a well-used red-dirt road, with deeply rutted tire tracks. Five miles further on they came to the small Zambian village of Siawaja. It was in Siawaja that they received their first hard bit of intel about the poachers and where they came from. When poaching gangs tore through their village, the scared and pissed-off locals would often complain to the park rangers. Tony and his team liked to involve the villagers, who were eyes on the ground, in the protection of the native wildlife that shared the surrounding countryside. They realized that the poorest communities on both sides of the border needed to be incentivized to avoid the lure of poaching and forged a mutually beneficial arrangement.

A scatter of stone-and-mud huts and tiny hole-in-the-wall stores made up the village that was bustling with chickens, goats, dogs and children. Passing a handful of beloved doe-eyed cows grazing outside the kraal, Ben was invited inside the hut of the village headman. They sat on the ground comfortably and entered into an *indaba*. After the headman rambled on about the weather, the price of goats, the pending harvest, the bride price for his eldest daughter and whether he was interested in considering it, Ben was finally able to ask about any strangers, other than himself and Tony, who had been through his village.

Once Ben had finished talking with the headman, much to Tony's annoyance, as etiquette had dictated the exclusion of him and his white face, he asked, 'So what did the belligerent old bastard say?'

Ben ignored his derision, chewing his lower lip with concern. 'A couple of truckloads, most of them Zambian. But,' he seemed perplexed, 'the leaders weren't.'

'What do you mean, the leaders weren't?' Tony dropped his indignant air, now more intrigued than irritated. 'Weren't what?'

'The ones who carried the guns, obviously, the poachers. The ones clearly doing the shooting,' Ben explained. 'He said they spoke like me, using Sindebele, they weren't Zambian. He also said he had seen many like them during the war.'

'Matabele? They were Matabele insurgents who fought during the war?'

'Basically, yes. But there was one Matabele, a ruthless, hard man that controlled them all.'

Tony's hunch proved true. 'Vusa,' he hissed. He now knew exactly who was coordinating the poaching in Zimbabwe's Zambezi Valley.

'The headman said he didn't go with his men, that he went back to the lake.'

'Obviously why he was alone when we came upon him,' Tony reasoned. 'But what about the trucks? If the main men were Matabele, does he know where they went? Back to Zim, possibly?'

'No, up to the Vic Falls to Choma Road, the Zambian T1. He said he heard them talking about heading north to Lusaka. He claimed they have been through his village many times.'

'Shit.' Tony heaved a heavy sigh. This was far worse than he had anticipated. This was well-coordinated and well-planned, far bigger and broader in scope than he had ever imagined. He knew Operation Stronghold was fully involved against trained and seasoned insurgents, fighting a battle of their own.

If they were going to catch this slippery kingpin, Tony insisted they had to hit the water immediately and go into action. Any delays could be disastrous, he reasoned. He and Ben made a dash to the parks service barge back to Kariba. The lake snaked through a labyrinth of riverine woodland. Cruising past hippos half-submerged in paddies of water hyacinth and showy weaver nests overhanging from branches like lanterns, the weaver birds announced their arrival.

They contemplated, discussing what they had learnt at Siawaja, as they scanned the red-sanded banks, where giant crocs were sunning themselves and canoe fishermen were unloading their catches.

But Ben thought Tony's haste and knee jerk reaction was a scattershot approach, and couldn't keep quiet for long. 'So what, you're going to head up to Lusaka and just ask around? "Hey, anyone here heard of Jacob Vusa?"' he mimicked, '"You know, the Matabele poaching kingpin? Lives round here somewhere."'

'Well, you do better,' Tony replied irritably. 'We have to get a lead on him somehow, track down the murdering bastard… fucking criminal.'

'Going in guns blazing won't get us any closer than we already are. Just remember, the Zambians have taken serious offense to Zimbabwe's policy of "shoot poachers on sight",' Ben air quoted. 'They class it as nothing short of licensed murder of Zambian citizens.'

'The bastard's not even Zambian, he's Matabele… a Zimbabwean citizen.'

'Moot point,' Ben fired back. 'To operate like he does, with impunity in Zambia, he'll have Zambian politicians in his back pocket. He won't be the only one getting fat from poaching rhino horn. A lot of people are going to have a vested interest in his success.'

'Yeah, I get it,' Tony groaned, but he knew Ben was right. 'Okay, Mr Diplomacy, what are our options? Normally, you're all for a direct approach. How come you've become so bloody righteous all of a sudden?'

'Nothing diplomatic or righteous about it. All we have to do is lure him back across the river, and we nab the bastard.'

'Really?' Tony cocked an interested eyebrow. 'And how do you propose we do that?'

Ben, constantly burning with ideas, had a conspirator's grin. 'Funny you should ask me that.' He laid out his plan before Tony, whose smile broadened with every sentence spoken.

Vusa's home was in the exclusive residential district of Sunningdale, near the center of Lusaka, adjacent to the city's golf club. While he was a member of the club, and conducted business there regularly, it was not a sport that he particularly enjoyed or participated in. He considered it too shamefully colonial and a stupid waste of time.

The property, spilling over five acres in a parkland setting, was dominated by an English mock-tutor homestead, complete with thatch-roof, black-hardwood trim and stark-white plaster stucco. It also had a quaint one-bedroom pool cottage for guests and staff quarters for five. It was the type of place that would have obvious appeal to an international smuggler and served as an ideal travel hub for his nefarious activities. His home, within five minutes of Lusaka's City Airport, allowed him easy access to a multitude of other regional destinations, some recognized, and others barely dirt strips in the middle of the bush. Crucially, it was a 120-mile hop by chartered plane to the Zimbabwean township of Kariba, right in the heart of his current poaching activities. Within ten minutes of landing at Kariba's airport, he could be at the boat ramp at Marinaland, launching his pontoon boat and motoring up the lake, to collect his latest accumulated booty from the carnage he wrought along Zimbabwe's Zambezi Valley.

As Vusa's enterprise was flush with horn from his latest haul, his main focus was processing it for maximum return. None of this was undertaken anywhere near his Sunningdale residence. He kept a distinct delineation between his personal and business affairs.

His warehousing complex was located in Lusaka's central business district, in the suburb of Northmead, behind the Northmead Market on Kanjila Road. It was a stone's throw from the Zambian police station and a slew of other government headquarters. When he paid his bribes, Vusa never liked to have to travel too far to do so.

Rimmed by barbed wire, the 5,000-square-foot warehouse was security fenced, with all employees checked in and out by armed security personnel. There were several bays to the central processing facility, with mezzanine offices above for Vusa and his plant manager, Shalan bin Yehaye Hbubari. Hbubari was a squint-eyed, hook-nosed Arab of slight build, whose flowery speech did nothing for the distrust Vusa quickly developed for the man.

Vusa hired Hbubari to oversee the manufacturing of his rhino horn *jambiya*, directly from the Yemenis capital of Sana'a. Until meeting Vusa, Hbubari had worked at Souk al Janabi, a centuries-old bazaar in the capital's Al Sabeen business district. It had been his and his family's place of business for many generations.

While *jambiya* sheaths and belts were also sold here, one part of the souk was home to the true artisans of the *jambiya* trade, the manufacture and craftsmanship of the blade's rhino-horn handles. These craftsmen tended to specialize in one of the five separate stages of the handles production. Working alongside his father, until his death, had given Hbubari an intimate working knowledge of all phases of this specialty craft. After an incident involving a neighbor's daughter, the manufacture of a particularly ornate *jambiya* and a bag of Yemeni gold coins, Hbubari accepted Vusa's offer.

Vusa only ever received a cryptic, long-winded explanation of why Hbubari accepted his offer so readily: 'Contrary to what many foreigners believe, a *jambiya* is a symbol of peace. For centuries they have been used to solve the conflicts of Yemeni tribes by submitting them to their chieftains for arbitration. At this point, the fight stops and the process of solution begins.' Vusa soon learnt that the chieftain he had to submit to was his neighbor, and the *jambiya* being submitted was the ornate blade in question, with the whereabouts of the bag of gold coins unknown. But he also learned that if he wished to purchase some authentic Yemeni gold coins, Hbubari had some for sale. It was at about this time that Vusa decided his security guards needed to watch Hbubari more than any other employee.

Hbubari had set up Vusa's manufacturing along traditional lines, of which he oversaw every facet of the horn-handle production. While initially an excruciatingly slow process, it seemed very little horn was discarded, needing to be ground into powder for the Asian market. He spent the bulk of his time overseeing the crafting of the *jambiyas* T-shaped handles.

Under intense scrutiny, the process began with locally trained craftsmen heating oblong sections of horn to make them pliable and easily workable. Once the desired shape was achieved, they were filed and polished with fine-grit sandpaper until a pale lustrous glow was achieved. Much like a jeweler, who would carefully collect all his bench filings and sweeps, Vusa ensured all filed horn was saved to be sold for so-called traditional "medicine".

Hbubari found that if he tightly controlled these 'local baboons', as he referred to them, out of Vusa's earshot, and had them repeatedly perform only one task, he could maintain quality and control of the finished product to his exacting demands.

Once the horn had been shaped and polished, a craftsman drilled tiny holes along its length and riveted in small pieces of ornate silver wire. A third tradesman then reheated the handle and reshaped it under Hbubari's direction. While it was still warm a damp cloth soaked in ash was applied to the surface and used to polish it again.

A fourth craftsman carefully cut a slit in the handle's base that eventually accepted the short, recurved double-edged blade. This craftsman also added decorative silver around the base, before fastening it and the blade to the handle with animal-hoof collagen glue. While the glue was setting, this craftsman drilled holes at the top and bottom of the handle for large decorative rivets that pinned either gold, copper or brass coins at each location. The plain brass coins Vusa sourced in Yemen, while embossed coins he imported from Egypt and Syria. But the best handles were decorated with two handmade Yemeni gold coins, sourced from none other than the resourceful Hbubari.

A fifth and final craftsman completed the finishing stage. He wiped and cleaned the handle, then with a mixture of powdered charcoal and candle wax he covered the central section to darken it.

Hbubari had seriously intimated to Vusa one day: 'A good *jambiya* handle has three colors, for morning, afternoon and night. The morning color is yellowish, signifying the rising of the sun. In the afternoon, it is green, showing off the midday glow of the waters of the Gulf of Aden. By night it deepens close to black, indicative of the darken Arabian heavens.' He further explained, 'The *jambiya* changes color because rhino horn is a creation of God. There is a spirit alive inside the horn, and thus inside the handle. It glows and changes colors with the mood of God.'

While the warehouse also had a blacksmithing shop, this section of manufacture was conducted in secret. From the village of Kawaza, located adjacent to the South Luangwa National Park in the west of Zambia, ancient descendants of the Kunda tribe have made their home there as ancient iron workers. When Vusa put it out among the populous of rural Zambia that he was looking for blacksmiths, it didn't take long for these artisans to show up at his door. Once they discovered what he desired, their only request was the supply of high-tensile steel, something he was able to supply from surplus Soviet military equipment. These may have been rural blacksmiths, but their end product rivaled, if not surpassed, the high-quality blades made predominantly in the Yemeni city of Dhamar.

The third aspect of manufacture, conducted at Vusa's processing plant, was from a purpose-built leather-working studio for the *Aseeb*, the *jambiya's* sheaths. It was the sheath that distinguishes the two main styles of *jambiya*. The common design was the *asib*, J-shaped with a noticeable crook at the belly of the J, worn by those claiming tribal origin. This design secures the *jambiya* behind the belt, but allows the blade to be quickly drawn, leaving the sheath in place. But it was the second style of sheath, reserved for the *qadis*, or judges, and those who claimed descendancy from the prophet Mohammed, that substantially escalated Vusa's profit. These select few were entitled to wear a different style of sheath called a *thusa*, which doesn't have a crook or hook at the bottom of the J. This sheath curves and is distinguishable by its *thuma*, a round knob at the top of the handle, instead of the T.

In all, Hbubari was able to complete the manufacture of Vusa's rhino-horn handles in just over three days of supervised workmanship, and he was never happier when blades were finished with the handmade Yemeni gold coins. These blades, whether styled as an *asib* or a *thuma*, were destined for sale to sheiks, Arabian princes and the ruling elite for extortionate prices.

It wasn't until Vusa landed his first consignment of *jambiya* to Yemen, under the guise of diplomatic reciprocity of trade with Burundi, that he began reaping the true profit potential of his far-sighted enterprise. Surreptitiously, he was invited to watch as his blades were put up for sale by a long-established and trusted Yemeni retailer, known to Hbubari and his family.

As the drawn-out bargaining began, discerning customers felt the weight and balance of the metal to the horn and studied the intricacies of the handle's designs. Having traipsed from merchant to merchant seeing many other *jambiyas*, they could see these blades were of exceptional quality. At that point the offers and counter-offers began echoing throughout the souk, going on for hours, sometimes days.

It hardly mattered that rhino-horn imports had been banned in Yemen, as *jambiyas* had been part of a Yemeni man's dress for centuries. Rhino horn had been considered the most prestigious material for a *jambiya* handle, and little has changed in Yemen heritage in this regard, it remains the most desirable substance for the dagger handles. The Yemenis have remained proud of their tribal traditions and long history, with westernization, its liberal values and conservationist sentiments being shunned.

Essentially, what Vusa had stumbled on and overcome was supplying a demand, but one steeped in the centuries-old tradition of a male's maniacal egocentricities.

Tony was frustrated at the slow progress they were making nabbing this poacher. They were really the last line of defense for the animals. Rhinos and elephants were dying in their thousands and arrests were few. Unless poachers were caught red-handed, poaching was difficult to prove. Hampering their efforts was the corruption that ran rife in the country and across the continent. When Tony and Ben reached Kariba after visiting the Zambian village headman, their first port of call was to a district magistrate whom he'd worked with during his years with Operation Stronghold. Tony wanted to know his legal position regarding an aggressive stance towards Vusa, before meeting with Glenn Tatum and discussing what he planned.

Edward Makomo was a Zimbabwean Shona, with the typical moon-faced features of his tribe, extenuated by good living, that contributed to his expansive belly. He was the resident magistrate with the Kariba Magistrates Court for the Province of Mashonaland West. But in relation to ZimParks and Operation Stronghold he was very familiar with all matters poaching and a strong advocate, prepared to prosecute those offenders to the letter of the law. His only disconcerting and annoying habit was that he carried a superior air of importance, reinforcing this with the frequent use of irrelevant legal terms in Latin, then repeating them in English.

'Tony, please come in.' Edward met him at the front door of his rough-cast home, just off Sable Drive in Kariba. He escorted him through to an outdoor dining area beside a pool with an artful infinity edge, overlooking the lake with the main Kariba ferry dock off to the side. In front of them, two acres of tropical garden tumbled down to the lakeshore. The dining area was positioned in the shade beneath the house's high-pitched thatched roof. Once they were both seated comfortably, he looked at Tony expectantly.

Tony came straight to the point. 'I assume you will have heard about the incident we had at the Stronghold holding pens at Msuna?'

'Yes, a terrible business. I would like to have the opportunity of seeing these criminals before my bench.'

Zimbabwe was known for its far-reaching legislation for its protection of wildlife, allowing for relatively severe prison sentences, particularly in cases where animals designated as "specially protected", such as the country's elephants and black rhinos. Tony knew Edward had fully prosecuted anyone convicted of illegally killing or hunting elephants or rhinos. He also knew convicted poachers were expected to compensate landowners for the value of the animals lost. And this was the area that Tony wanted to discuss with him.

'We lost 25 adult rhinos and seven calves, and I believe the economic loss to ZimParks will be significant.'

'Yes, you are correct. The compensation due per animals will be *ad valorem*, in proportion to their value, and could run in the hundreds of thousands of dollars for just one animal. This would be in the vicinity of the judgment I would impose,' Edward confirmed, then mournfully shaking his head, added, 'But, sadly, most poachers are desperately poor, with little ability to offer any sort of compensation. In reality, the application of the law in cases like this most recent act is uneven. Suspected poachers and ringleaders are regularly released on bail and simply disappear. The bottom line is that the laws are good, but the application can be very weak.'

'And if I was able to bring a suspected ringleader before you, who has substantial assets held in both Zimbabwe and Zambia, would you be able to successfully prosecute and hold him without him being able to flee?' Tony could see he had the magistrate's attention.

'Definitely.' Edward nodded. 'However, we would need to take a two or even three-pronged approach, both civil and criminal. *Prima facie*, on the face of it, if he was initially charged with poaching. And *per quod*, whereby, it was prosecuted as a civil matter, with a judgement ruled for the plaintiff, in this case ZimParks, the court could bring forth an enforcement of judgement for the execution of property, with civil imprisonment. Essentially a writ of execution could be issued against the defendant's movable, immovable, known and unknown property, aka his assets. The writ would need to show the defendant was a flight risk and had the ability to abscond.'

He paused, waiting for any questions, but Tony just nodded.

He puffed himself up and continued, 'This is where the second part of enforcement would be critical, the civil imprisonment. Compelling him to satisfy the judgement. But I must stress, civil imprisonment is only available where it is proven the defendant has the ability to pay and that his failure to do so is willful. Essentially you will need to show the court that he has assets, and they are currently beyond the court's reach.'

Tony considered this, knowing that Vusa's Zimbabwean and Zambian assets may be difficult to establish, let alone prove the existence of. He would face this problem if and when it became an issue.

When Tony never voiced his concerns, Edward continued, 'If this type of approach can be taken, as long as it is genuine, then huge compensation could definitely be levied and recovered for ZimParks, even taking into consideration the third phase, the criminal charges additionally being litigated, whether they run concurrently or even after the fact.' He paused for a second and looked inquiringly at Tony. 'This wouldn't have anything to do with that pontoon boat you attempted to seize recently, would it?'

'Yes, the one that was released,' Tony admitted bitterly. 'I believe it to be owned by the man responsible, whom I have been alluding to. A Matabele, ex-ZIPRA, living and operating from Lusaka.'

'Well, tribalism aside, I would be most interested to have this man before me. Yes, I believe there is something we can do here.'

Tony thanked him and went off to his meeting with Glenn Tatum.

Only a week after the police investigation and burying their murdered comrades and the rhinos, the Stronghold rangers were redoubling their efforts to protect the animals at the other three stockades. During the morning meeting, Tony, Ben, Glenn and Andy were hashing out the next move in Andy's quirky, colorful office at the ranger station.

On a wall, beneath a window, sat a wooden shelf heaving with worn nature books and little curiosities, a model of the yellow Moth biplane from the previous summer's film *Out of Africa*, and Andy's eclectic finds, a sun-bleached giant African snail shell, a painted ostrich egg, exotic bird plumes and porcupine quills. Hanging behind his desk was a large framed black-and-white Peter Beard photo of a pair of cheetah cubs staring forlornly across the plains. Another Beard print of a sultry black model standing naked, hand-feeding a giraffe in the bush.

But it was the large-scale map of Lake Kariba and the Zambezi Valley, pinned on the back wall, that held everyone's attention. The four men stood staring at the map and discussing Operation Crash, so-named after the alternate word for a herd of rhinos.

'I don't like it. I don't like it at all,' Glenn said, full of concern. 'It's a helluva risk.'

Tony dove straight in, 'I understand that. But the only way we have any hope of stopping him is if we catch him on Zim soil… *again*,' he added pointedly. 'You know we have no jurisdiction in Zambia.'

Glenn turned slowly and shot him a stone-cold stare. At times like this his previous military training and bearing was clear. 'I appreciate that, but it still doesn't diminish the risk.'

'Yes, I know, but it's our chance to shut him down.'

'Um, Tony is right,' Ben said in solidarity. Glenn turned and stared down at the diminutive Matabele tracker, who stood his ground. 'I have spoken to the headman across the river. And I believe they will once again use his village as the staging point, before making the crossing, with him being prepared to tip us off of their arrival and numbers.'

Glenn looked back at the map again as he considered this information. He had been involved with the park service for nearly two decades and knew only too well the limits of their powers. The Zambezi Valley was too vast for the rangers to protect and surrounded by impoverished villages across the river and a porous border, and their resources were already stretched. He was very cautious and liked to do everything by the book, which sometimes drove Tony mad.

'But how can we be so sure this Vusa will come across the lake from Zambia again?'

'The headman will inform us,' Tony answered.

'And on the Zimbabwean side? How do we know if he leads the poachers on the raid?'

'We believe they will land again somewhere along the corridor. There are only so many secure landing spots, which we will stake out with well-concealed hides,' Tony said, glancing at Ben. 'Ben and I can set up hides at the likely location, man them with our own teams and keep in radio contact with each other. We'll know exactly when and where they land, and if Vusa is with them. Andy and I will set up our welcoming committee accordingly.'

Glenn looked accusingly at Andy, who stood quietly beside him, saying little. 'You've discussed this, and agree with the plan?'

'Yes, sir,' the Mana Pools warden said in acknowledgment. Andy, like Tony, was a renegade, but he thought this was Tony's plan and he needed to take responsibility for it.

'Huh,' Glenn grunted, 'seems like it's all arranged.' Yet it was clear he still had reservations. 'But grouping together and relocating all our captured rhinos to the holding pens above the Msuna camp is a huge, huge risk. That's nearly a hundred animals, gentleman. How can you guarantee their safety? After all, we've hardly recovered from last week's devastating hit.' His eyes sweeping from Andy to Ben and lastly to Tony, who answered.

'We have just under a hundred trained rangers, all wanting a crack at the bastards who killed their colleagues. If we used half of them, we could set up an ambush in front of the holding pens, and bring in a stop line once Vusa has brought his men past this point.' Tony stepped up to the map and pointed to two locations on it. 'Here and here. They won't be able to reach the pens, or escape back to the river, without going back through our stop line.'

Glenn still wasn't convinced. 'And how will he know the rhinos have been relocated?'

'We believe he has people on this side of the border in his pay. We will ensure that it becomes public knowledge.' Tony could feel his boss slowly allowing himself to be persuaded.

'And you say you've spoken to the magistrate?'

'Yes. He will be happy to throw the book at Vusa and extract compensation for ZimParks accordingly.'

Glenn was silent for a long time as he mulled it over. 'Okay, get it done.'

'Yes, sir. We'll definitely get it done.' He relished getting another crack at Vusa before he left, hopefully in a blaze of glory.

As Tony, with Ben at his side, turned to leave, Glenn thrust an accusing finger at him. 'Don't fuck this up and leave us with a bloody mess to clean up… especially after you and Ben have buggered off, working for the WWF.'

CHAPTER 5

The Bush Welcoming Committee

OPERATION STRONGHOLD HAD four main holding stockades for the black rhinos captured in the Zambezi Valley. But after the raid on the holding pens at Msuna, only three others still held adults and calves waiting for relocation. Mana Pools had the largest number, followed by those at the Matusadona National Park on the southern shore of Lake Kariba, and a smaller one located in the Sijarira Forest Area. All three holding areas were a hive of activity, readying their rhinos for transportation to Msuna. It was a colossal effort. All the adults and larger adolescents needed to be tranquilized and loaded on board the waiting trucks, ensuring that family groups were kept together, with the smaller calves carefully handled and bundled onboard with their mothers. With all trucks loaded at Mana Pools needing to take Zimbabwe's A1 south, the township of Kariba was soon awash with the buzz of all the goings-on.

Of equally frenzied activity were Tony and Ben along the banks of the Zambezi, setting up the observation hides above those beachheads on the Zimbabwean side of the corridor where the poachers were likely to land. Tony wanted these hides set up and concealed well in advance of all the rhinos arriving at his Msuna holding pens. They chose four likely spots along the corridor that he felt would be ideal landing beachheads for the number of poachers and porters needed for a raid on over 80 animals. While they took special pains to conceal the hides from discovery from the river, each one was interconnected with the others by recently cut-out pathways concealed through the jesse and valley's bush. Tony wanted all his men available to engage what he suspected would be a sizable poaching force.

'Okay, Fredrick Selous,' Tony said to Ben sarcastically, using the name of the famous African hunter and guide. 'I can still see two of the hides. They need to be concealed better.' He had canoed down the Zambezi, the full length of the corridor, trying to identify where the four hides that Ben had positioned above the beaches they suspected the poachers would use.

'But it'll be night when they land,' Ben tried hopefully. It was a long traipse through the bush back to the hides Tony had seen. He knew which ones they were; they were the last two. Ben had tried to skimp on material to lessen his burden of carrying it through the bush.

'Just do it,' Tony snapped. 'I need to check on the progress up at the contact zone. Get the canoe back up the river. I want one last look at all four hides before dark this evening.'

As they stood at the dock below their Msuna camp, Ben groaned in exasperation.

'Sorry what?' Tony pointedly held a hand up to his ear when he'd heard his grumbling.

'I said that's a 29-mile hike back up river through the bush.' But Ben knew there was no point, he put it down to Tony being in one of his defiant moods where he would never take no for an answer. He turned to the two porters standing behind them and told them to head with the canoe back up through the bush again. He would grab some more canvas to help conceal the two supposedly patchy hides. He mumbled something about being underappreciated and significantly underpaid, before heading for the canvas.

Tony wasn't listening. He knew how good this bastard Vusa was and everything had to be on point to even have a chance of luring him successfully into the trap. He headed to his Land Rover so he could drive up to the holding pens. Once up there he would walk down the short distance to where he had positioned the contact zone, the site of his ambush, to ensure there were no signs in front of it to give away its concealed location. Vusa would be as wary as a fox approaching a henhouse. And Tony needed to offer as clear and open invitation as possible so that he could swing the gate closed behind him and his gang of murderous thugs with the stop line that would seal the trap.

'Howzit, Andy?' Tony asked once he jumped out of his Land Rover, and walked from the holding pens down to the tree line that ringed the stockade.

'Good. But man, I hope we get word soon from across the river.' Then Andy explained his misgivings. 'It's only a couple of days before the full moon, the scene will be lit up like a bushbuck in the headlights.' He motioned vaguely to the new earthworks below the ambush site's trench line. 'It's going to be hard to conceal that, especially as they'll be coming up the hill towards it.'

In front of the trees was a bushed-lined clearing that the poachers would have to cross before getting up into the trees that ringed the holding stockade.

'Okay, we've heard nothing yet from the headman at Siawaja,' Tony answered, 'We'll have to hope for plenty of cloud cover on the night of the raid. Otherwise the moon will definitely light us up as if it's day.'

'Yeah, that's the worry.'

Tony looked at the newly dug soil. 'We'll have to spread it down the hill, so the mounds don't look out of place.' He looked up at the sky, clouds were forming overhead, there would be rain this afternoon. 'Get your boys on to it now. The rain can help wash it away.'

There was nothing that Tony could do about the full moon, but there were a whole raft of other issues that he had to solve. He had worked with Andy during the war and there was a good accord between them, especially for this type of work, carried over from their time as reservist warrant officers in the Rhodesian African Rifles. His next issue was to organize how he could conceal and bring up the stop line, before the poachers were engaged out in the open. For this he knew he'd need Ben's help, the little tracker would know how and where to conceal those rangers needed to cut off the poachers escape. He needed to get back to him, he would soon have the canoe waiting.

The lone rhino bull watched warily from his hideout of scrubby bush and trees, his flanks glistening in mud, his nostrils quivering as he caught the alien scents. He had been spooked by all this coming and going, didn't like it one bit. Ever since that large body of men had come through his domain from the river and gone back the same way, there had been the stench of death lingering like a pungent odor, hanging about the bush. And now there had been new trails hacked into the jesse bush, linking up a number of beaches along the river.

He wasn't prepared to emerge out of his dense tangle of bush for his nightly drink. Luckily it had rained and there were scattered puddles of brackish water that he was able to drink from, as his routine of venturing down to the river to slack his thirst had been interrupted. Every one of the beaches that he used seemed to now be tainted with that acrid reek of man. He had stealthily investigated two of these beaches, and on each of them above the pathways he used to get down to the water were alien structures or some sort of shelters built that looked out over the water. The only routine that hadn't been interrupted was the daily use of his dunghill, located deep in one particularly dense patch of jesse bush further up the slope.

He stepped well off the path he was on. He'd once again heard movement coming towards him, up one of these newly hacked pathways. He smelt more than saw the men. There were two of them and they were carrying something, like a hollowed-out log or half of a giant gourd, chirping and grunting in that disconcerting way that they used to communicate. He would have moved back to the pathway to get away from this beach, when he heard another of these bipods coming. He was alone, but stopped at the foreign structure, spread some sort of covering over it, spent time hacking more branches from the trees around it, dragging and stacking them over it, then hurried away. He appeared to be quietly bleating or mumbling to himself as he walked away.

No, he didn't like it, especially as it was daylight, and he was starting to get annoyed. Stealthily moving back on to the pathway, he would keep well behind this one, the last of the three men. Up ahead the pathway dissected a game trail that he would use to melt further back into the bush.

CHAPTER 6

Moving Giants

DOUGLAS TANAKA, A sly old Shona rogue, liked to poke his nose into everyone's business. He was about 65, weathered and dried out like an ancient stick of tobacco, and as stooped as a marabou stork. He was dubiously related to one of Vusa's Kunda blacksmiths, by way of a recent union with one of the blacksmith's distant cousins. The cousin was his fourth wife. She was the flowering of his aged and withered heart, the light in his otherwise glassy and fading eyes. She was so full of energy, laughter and joy, and was his little laughing dove, his njiwa in Swahili, the common language they shared. And the old man doted on her. While these sort of intertribal marriages weren't uncommon, Tanaka's lifestyle was always a source of regular and intriguing information that once imparted gave him standing that he wouldn't normally receive from outside of his own tribal circles.

Once Vusa became aware of Tanaka's existence and since he had an association with an already committed employee on his retainer, the employee earned certain favors by passing on the old man's information directly to him.

The bent old Shona was a familiar presence at Mana Pools, regularly used by ZimParks as a truck driver to transport the relocated rhinos to protected sanctuaries across Zimbabwe. Since Vusa's warehouse complex was only three hours by road to the border crossing at the Kariba Dam, Tanaka was able to make weekly visits to his wife and her extended family, and impart all that he had gleaned from his week across the border in Zimbabwe.

The Shona's gossip spread on the African grapevine. Once it made its way to Vusa, he had summoned the old man to his mezzanine office in the warehouse. One of the reasons his shady enterprise thrived for so long was because of his network of spies and paid-for allegiance of local informants.

His hard, calculating eyes settled on the old Shona. 'Tell me about the transportation of the Zimbabwean rhino,' he asked Tanaka in Swahili, their common language.

'*Bwana mkubwa*, great lord,' Tanaka began flattering him. 'There has been much coming and going with trucks from Mana Pools, Matusadona and Sijarira, to the holding depot at Msuna.' Then added for emphasis. 'I have seen these things with my very own eyes.'

This was indeed interesting news. He studied the old man's milky eyes. 'How many trucks?'

'A great, great many.' Tanaka broke into his shifty toothless grin, trying to hide his ignorance. In reality he had only been involved with those shipments coming out of Mana Pools and hadn't seen much else.

Vusa took this in his stride. In Tanaka's telling, the holding pens were stacked to the rafters with rhinos. He suspected the old man was semi-illiterate and would have difficulty counting past 20. 'How many trips were you involved with?' Mana Pools to Msuna was a round-trip of 18 hours, but with loading and unloading it was realistically a two-day trip.

'For two weeks, I have been involved. Today is my first break since they began trucking the *faru*, the rhino, from there.'

'How many other trucks?' Vusa asked, veiling his growing excitement. This was beginning to sound like a large undertaking.

'Myself and five others.' What Tanaka failed to mention that for three days of these two weeks he was broken down at Mana Pools.

This was starting to sound better and better. That could be close to 35 or 40 rhinos, Vusa realized. 'How many are now held at Msuna?'

Tanaka began rubbing his wispy grey goatee indecisively and picked his nose while he thought about what to say. He hadn't been back to Msuna since his truck had been repaired at the Mana Pools workshop. He wiped the remnant of dried snot on his trousers before answering. 'Ah… a great, great many.' He had heard they had finished loading at Matusadona and Sijarira, and perhaps there were only a few more trips to come out of Mana Pools.

'But how many rhinos did you see?'

'I think now there may be 100 held there,' he hazarded a guess. 'Once we have finished with those from Mana Pools, we begin relocating them throughout Zimbabwe.'

Vusa was staggered at the number and realized he could make a killing. He calculated quickly. This could be close to a thousand pounds of horn, and his warehouse was still busy, and would be for many more months from the last raid at Msuna. A haul like this was far too big to at least not investigate. This could keep production going for six months, maybe even a year. *But why?* he then suspiciously questioned. *Why Msuna and why now, especially after the last massive raid I just pulled off there?*

He continued prodding him for details, but didn't hold out much hope of getting a straight answer out of the toothless old rogue. 'Why, why now?' He was surprised with the answer he received.

'As there are no rhinos left in the Msuna area,' Tanaka began, 'and as *Bosi* Tony and his *piccanin* Matabele tracker are…' He realized he was speaking to someone of the same tribe, but didn't know how to take back the derogatory remark, so instead hurried on, 'Um… are leaving Operation Stronghold. ZimParks wishes only to use the pens one last time before abandoning them and the camp for good. I have also heard it spoken thus,' the old man composed himself, before imparting his next gem of wisdom, 'Msuna is the southernmost holding depot and the shortest distance to the new protected sanctuaries they are taking the rhinos to. I myself know this to be true. I have driven from there many times.'

Vusa knew the close proximity of Msuna to the new sanctuaries was correct. He had already started scouting out these protected sanctuaries. When he had cleaned out the last of the rhinos from the Zambezi Valley, he would begin hitting those. He also knew the corridor had been heavily poached, especially as it was used so regularly for the infiltration and departure of his gangs. But as the parks service kept an accurate tally of all animals on the ground, this sounded like they were abandoning the location as it was no longer a viable protection area. This wasn't good. Maybe his poaching gangs had been too efficient with their relentless raids. And if Msuna was closing down, how far would his gangs have to travel to get among viable rhino populations again? Maybe he would have to begin infiltrating his men directly across the lake instead of up the river.

This in and of itself carried a whole raft of other problematic issues. The landing of so many men among the high gorge of the river easily concealed them, but out in the open, on the banks of Lake Kariba? This would attract attention.

He noticed the old Shona had been curiously watching him as he contemplated what he'd been told. He needed to get rid of this old fool and think through what he had learned. 'You have given me much to think about, old grandfather,' he appeared to intone respectfully. 'Leave me now. Return in one week with more information.' He gave him a bit of money and dismissed the old man before calling for his poaching lieutenant. This accumulation of rhino at Msuna maybe too good to pass up, whether that bastard Tony Campbell was present or not.

Vusa's poaching lieutenant, Joseph Mehluki, literally meaning conqueror, was a battle-hardened Matabele warrior. He had fought as a ZIPRA soldier and knew nothing other than the way of the gun. He was just as disillusioned as Vusa with the new Zimbabwean government. He had also been cast aside, and turned back to the only thing he knew, killing. Vusa had kept him employed since becoming his man.

'I see you, *inkosi enkulu*, great lord,' Mehluki addressed Vusa in Sindebele, as he came to stand before him. Although he was a tall man, able to look Vusa squarely in the eye, he bowed his head of peppercorn curls and kept his eyes downcast. When Vusa acknowledged him, he still kept his gaze lowered to hide the hideous scar that pulled one side of his face askew. The ugly cicatrix that ran down from his brow to his chin was caused by a phosphorous grenade, thrown among a group of insurgents he had been leading during the bitter bush war.

'How is it with you, Mehluki?' Vusa asked before coming to the heart of the reason he called the meeting with his lieutenant. 'Are the men rested?'

Mehluki looked up wolfishly for a fleeting second at his boss. 'They are well rested.' His whole face twisted out of shape as he smiled.

'Then I may have work for all of you. If what I am planning works out, I will want ten separate teams this time. Each gun-boy to have four porters. Do we have enough comrades who are trained?' Vusa knew it would be a large group, possibly 40 men, but it sounded like he could put every one of them to work.

'We have nine *inkosi*. There was a need for discipline, one of the gun-boys now has a broken arm and will have trouble walking for a number of weeks.' Mehluki shrugged, suggesting these things happened.

'Anything I need to know?' Vusa was very wary about upsetting the delicate balance that he paid for to keep the locals happy.

'There was an incident with a woman.' Mehluki shrugged again. 'But the matter is now settled.'

Vusa wasn't really listening now. There were always incidences with local women. But one gun-boy down was a problem. Then he realized it was probably the excuse he had been looking for. After all, it could be a big haul, and he would need to take maximum advantage of it. 'I can run the tenth team,' he decided, voicing his decision.

Mehluki looked at him again, the wolfish grin now resembling more of an approving if somewhat lopsided smile. While it hadn't happen regularly, the last raid being the first for many years, he liked it when his boss took control in the field. Plans went off without a hitch, the killing was always merciless, the spoils bountiful and the profits great.

'You were with me when I led the last raid on Msuna and you know the area. We may be going back there again. And if we do, this time, we will have the light of the full moon to easily illuminate the way, and we will kill many, many more *ubhejane*, rhino. But first you and I will need to go in alone.'

CHAPTER 7

The Trap is Set at Msuna

THE LAST OF the rhinos would be trucked up from Mana Pools to Msuna and arrive before sundown that afternoon. In all, there would be 86 adults and calves. The holding pens capacity had been stretched to their limit, and the parks service would soon need to start relocating the rhinos to avoid any harm coming to them. Tony was confident his preparations were complete, and he was in readiness for what he believed was the poachers' imminent raid.

He had shot down the Zambezi River in the canoe one last time and was happy that the prepared hides were invisible to casual observation, during the night they would be even more so. The two main issues were keeping the rangers to be used in the stop line hidden, but ready to close off the poachers escape, and disguising the earthworks thrown up by the trenching in the trees below the holding pens.

'I don't like it.' Tony stood with his hands on hips, in the clearing below the trees, looking up at the prepared position. He had just come up from the Msuna dock by Land Rover after canoeing down the river. Even though it had rained the day before, new earth was still visible among the trees. He was worried by how bright it would be with the light cast by the full moon.

'Tony,' Ben began to give his opinion, 'the poachers will have had a hard slog up through the bush, and will be otherwise occupied by the time they get here. You know what to look for, they won't. I also think that it'll rain again this afternoon. Most of the dirt will be washed in by then.'

Tony reluctantly accepted Ben's assertion, but didn't want to draw attention to the two of them standing in the clearing, looking up at the trees. He signaled Ben with a nod to follow him. Slowly the two crept into the tangle of trees and undergrowth, hidden among the shadows. Hearing vehicles approaching, they both looked down the hill to the road snaking its way up to the pens. There were two park service trucks grinding their way up the grade, leaving a trail of dust like smoke behind them. These would be the last two from Mana Pools. One truck parked in the layby at the top of the hill, and after the dust cloud had washed over it, the other reversed straight up to the loading ramp to offload the animals from its padded crate.

'Who do we have here?' Tony muttered, sinking further back into the gloom of the trees.

There was an old skinny black man, with a scruff of a goatee, alight from the driver's seat, and two tall, presumably, assistants from the passenger's side. The only problem was, there wasn't supposed to be anyone else in the truck except the driver. One individual stood out among them.

'Vusa,' Tony groaned when he saw him getting out of the truck.

'And his henchman,' Ben said, looking at the other man. 'I know him. He was a ZIPRA commander during the war. He is Matabele, but cares nothing for the land of his birth. He's a very hard man, rotten to the core, and one we will need to keep a close eye on before this is over.'

They watched both men walk up to the holding pens, climb to the top rail and begin looking at the accumulation of animals held in front of them.

'Pretty-looking fellow,' Tony said, glimpsing the man's badly scarred face. 'Does he have a name?'

'Joseph Mehluki. His father's kraal is two miles away from my uncle's, on the outskirts of Hwange. He will know this area very well,' Ben said by way of explanation. 'He was recruited into ZIPRA as a child. His family thought he had been killed during the war until he turned up out of the blue, fully grown but scarred, after independence. And now has obviously switched to poaching, judging by his company.' Ben was looking from Mehluki to Vusa. 'They're obviously here to check that the rumors about all the rhinos are true. But we have to prevent them from coming down into these trees, if they do they'll realize it's a trap.'

'We need to distract them.' Tony scanned around and quickly decided. 'This is what we'll do…'

Vusa and Mehluki had made the reconnaissance trip from Lusaka down the Zambian T1 to the border crossing at Victoria Falls, using his Zambian-registered Land Rover. They had no issues crossing the border and making their way further down onto the Zimbabwean A8. They turned left at the Dete Crossroad, and made their way to the small lakeside village of Mlibizi. There they waited to meet Douglas Tanaka at the side road to Msuna, just down from the village's ferry dock. The old Shona was true to his word, if but for a few hours, and apologetically took them on board his truck and up the remaining ten miles to the ZimParks pens. Tanaka assured Vusa there would be no problems getting him and Mehluki to the stockades, so they could see the rhinos. There appeared to be little security the last few times he had been there.

Until Vusa was standing on the holding pen's railings, he didn't truly believe what he'd been told. But now, while numbers may be slightly less than the hundred animals Tanaka had indicated, he couldn't hardly credit what he was seeing. There was definitely a great harvest waiting to be reaped. Now looking around there seemed to be a few rangers but nothing to warrant concern over. It appeared Tanaka was correct about the limited security presence. Yet he needed to be sure.

Just as Vusa was about to walk to the tree line to survey the best route up from the river, the skies opened up. Caught in the downpour, the three men were forced to hurriedly seek cover back in the truck.

'We will wait for the rain to stop,' Vusa said to his lieutenant once they were back in the cab, peering out through now rapidly fogging windows. 'Then we will scout—'

Before he could finish his sentence, he saw the vague outline of a vehicle pull up beside the driver's side door. There was an urgent peeling on the horn and a series of yelled commands.

'It is *Bosi* Tony,' Tanaka quailed nervously, unsure of what to do. He had had only one other dealing with Tony in the past, and he still vividly recalled the unnerving and thoroughly unmanning incident as if it were yesterday.

Several months back Tony was assisting with the relocation of captured rhinos from Mana Pools. Tanaka had neglectfully caused one of the rhinos to badly tear its hide when he hadn't properly secured one of the holding pen's sharpened locking pins on his truck. Tony had witnessed the incident and when he saw the severity of the injury he had flown into a towering rage at Tanaka's carelessness. It appeared he would have taken the *sjambok* whip he carried to him if his Matabele tracker hadn't intervened. However, he still received a scathing dressing down and dock in pay. He was literally in awe and more than a little frightened of that white man and his rage.

Tony had run through the trees to the other side of the stockade to where he'd left his Land Rover. He left Ben in the trees watching the truck and its occupants. He reached his vehicle just as the rain started up again. He drove back around the pens, blasting his horn, and slowed to a stop beside Tanaka's truck.

He wound down his window and yelled, 'Hey, you lazy bastard, it's only water. Get out of the truck and unload these rhinos.'

'Do it,' hissed Vusa, as he and Mehluki sank down below the line of the windows. He could see, even though it was still raining, Campbell had got out of his vehicle and was slapping his palm on the driver's door, then he ran to the back of the truck.

Tanaka, flushed with worry, still hesitated. 'Get out,' Vusa barked at him, 'before I throw you out.'

Tanaka hurriedly rushed into the rain, doing as he was told.

Vusa and his lieutenant made no move to try and see what was happening, but hunkered down in their seats. There was a lot of shouting and banging, with the truck wildly rocking back and forth, but nobody seemed to be aware of their presence in the cab. Then, in a heart-stopping moment, the driver's door was wrenched open, but out of the rain, thankfully, it was only a very wet and sopping Tanaka who jumped up onto the seat. He slammed the door but before he could say anything, there was an insistent pounding on the door, and a yelled command to wind down the window. When Tanaka hesitated, with the tension building inside the cab like a pressure gauge in the red, Vusa sinking even lower, viciously hissed again, 'Do it, you old fool, before he opens the door!'

Opening the window a crack, Tanaka peered down. His next words left no doubt as to who was there. 'Yes, *Bosi* Tony,' he said with a sickly expression splashed across his sodden face.

'Go back to Mana Pools and wait for orders,' Tony commanded. 'We begin shipping these animals south in three days' time. Now go!'

'Yes, *Bosi*.' Tanaka started the truck and would have pulled away, but he over-revved the engine and with a lurch stalled it dead. He gave a whinnying laugh, briefly shooting a nervous smile down at Tony, who was now standing irritably, with his hands on his hips, waiting for him to leave. Tanaka frantically reached for the keys, nearly flooded the motor, but with an almighty backfiring fart, managed to start the truck again. This time, after loudly grating the gears, bunny-hopping forward twice, he finally pulled away.

Still cringing down in his seat, muttering foully, Vusa vowed to discipline the old Shona fool at the very next opportunity. That had been far too close for comfort.

'And that gets rid of you,' Tony said of Vusa and the departing truck as it snaked down the curving hill. He knew Vusa hadn't seen any of his preparations among the tree line, but did hopefully now believe if he wanted the rhinos held at Msuna he would have to work to a shortened timeline. Tony was confident he would be seeing Vusa back within a few short days.

CHAPTER 8

The Raiding Party

It was a hurried ten-hour trip back to Lusaka for Vusa and Mehluki. By the time they reached the Zambian capital, it was already midnight. There was very little to discuss during their trip, both Mehluki and Vusa already knew the lay of the land, and Tony Campbell's voice still rung clearly in Vusa's head. He had three days, or more precisely now, two and a half, before the rhinos started to be shipped out of Msuna. Just enough time he suspected to mobilize his men, get them in position, hit the stockades, harvest the horn, and be gone before any animals were beyond his reach.

Even though it was the middle of the night, there was a frenzy of activity once he got back to Lusaka. He knew virtually half the criminal underworld of southern Africa but was short of time. Quickly he had Mehluki rouse and organize all the Matabele poachers, his gun-boys, and the Zambian porters. It may have been unfair to call these harden Matabele insurgents the diminutive "boy". Yet they accepted the title with pride as it was an old and recognized term that elevated them far above the lowly porters that serviced them and the carnage they wrought. Vusa instructed his lieutenant to use those Zambian porters that were on the recent raid, but as this would still leave them short on numbers, to find others they had used in the past, so these men would be familiar with how they operated. He would have preferred to gather all the men well in advance, but as there was little time if they were left short of manpower, so be it. If necessary, the outgoing load would have to be apportioned across the whole group.

Next, he went over all the weapons himself. This was a task he always performed before any raid. He not only wanted all his Matabele well-armed, with plenty of ammunition, but wanted them with no excuse to kill and keep killing until there was nothing left alive to shoot.

Once all was in readiness, Vusa had three canvas-covered flatbed trucks fueled, loaded with the men and weapons, and ready to depart. Due to the short notice, Mehluki was only able to gather 26 porters. In total, including himself, the group was made up of 36 men, with them to be distributed evenly across the trucks.

'It will have to do. The gun-boys can carry the load as well.' Vusa knew being Matabele they wouldn't like it, thinking it was beneath them, but as he would be present nobody would dare argue with him. 'Head to the village at Siawaja. I will fly to Kariba and bring up the pontoon boat.' He looked at his watch. It had taken them a further 12 hours to get to this stage. 'You will be there in eight or nine hours, just on dark. I will meet you there. Keep all the men in check. We will load immediately as soon as I arrive and then cross the river. Now go,' he ordered. He had a plane to charter.

As soon as Vusa left Msuna in the first truck, and the final one had unloaded and departed, a cordon was thrown up around the stockades. No one was allowed in or out, preventing what was planned from being leaked to the outside world and especially to Vusa.

Once the lockdown was in place, Tony called up all those ZimParks rangers who were to be involved, assembling them in the parking area in front of the stockades, informing the massed congregation for the first time what their mission truly was. He could see and hear, by the nodding heads and murmured approvals, that they liked what they heard. They were keen to strike back at what most considered a heinous crime on the rhinos under their protection, but also an attack against them personally. He finalized their plans, making all the section heads repeat their call signs and orders, ensuring all the men knew what was expected of them. As those rangers selected all had military experience and were armed to the teeth, Tony coordinated the mission as if it was a wartime operation, which it surely was.

In the end, Tony split his force. Half of the men were to be placed in ambush along the newly dug trenches among the trees below the pens, the other half were to be brought up as the stop line once the poachers had passed the point of no return. Andy Woodward would be in charge at the ambush site, while Tony would initially be in one of the hides, waiting for the poachers to make their landing. Depending on which beachhead they used, he would trail them and then coordinate the positioning of the rangers in the stop line. He had chosen the most likely landing spot to wait, with Ben taking up the next most probable one. As Tony had given no indication to Vusa during his previous arrest and seizure of his boat that they now knew how his gangs arrived and left the corridor, both he and Ben agreed. Due to the shortened timeline after Vusa's stockade visit, they felt he would probably with full confidence, use the same beach as the poachers had done before. As

Ben would be downriver, if they did pass his position, he would jump ahead and quickly be at Tony's side. The other two hides were located upriver, manned by two of Tony's top rangers, so if the poachers happened to also pass his position they would leapfrog up the valley until the poachers landing was made. Once all Vusa's men had feet on the ground, he and Ben would begin the task of secretly trailing them up towards the rhino stockades.

Tony and Ben had carefully gone over the ground and the most likely trails the poachers would use. They had chosen the stop line's holding position with care, concealing it well off to the flank, but within easy call. These men, in particular, would be on cold hard food rations for the duration of the mission, with no fires or cigarettes allowed that could give away their presence. Once Ben had determined the poachers' line of spore, the stop line, like closing a gate, would be brought up and set in place behind them.

While he felt Vusa wouldn't land his men tonight, expecting them to hit the stockade the following evening, he wanted everything in readiness and all men prepared in case Vusa did have his men waiting across the river. But as Ben hadn't been radioed from the headman at Siawaja, this reinforced his belief that it wouldn't be until tomorrow.

Tony was confident that the raid would happen, but now that the waiting had begun he was assailed with doubts. *Would Vusa come, or would he just send in his lackeys?*

While Tony was heartened that Vusa had personally inspected the stockades, he just wished he could be certain the bastard would come. If he didn't, they may destroy his gang, but Tony knew he would be free to rebuild and begin again, sending Zimbabwe's rhino hurtling to a sure and lasting extinction.

The first night, as expected, was uneventful. All night the team lay in wait, straining to listen to every sound. Tony left his two rangers at the first two hides, with instructions to radio in the unlikely eventuality that the poacher's boat was spotted, coming on for a daytime raid. Then, for the rest of the day, he inspected his preparations, making adjustments where necessary, as well as visiting all the men. Those that weren't sleeping, he teased and jollied them along, acknowledging the men he knew and introducing himself to those he didn't. He knew he needed them in high spirits and vigilant for the night's action ahead.

'I'll tell you one thing,' he told them, 'it will be tonight.' He could feel it in his bones. He had an intuitiveness, a sort of sixth sense, that bordered on the psychic.

It was now his second night's vigil and Tony was in his hide. He had done everything possible to ensure his mission's success. He glanced wearily at the shadowy trees and dark forest beyond. It was just on dusk and the hush of evening, like the quiet stalking of death, enveloped the surrounding bush and river. With the daytime sounds, chased away were the redden hues previously slashed through the distant heavens. It seemed like it wasn't only him waiting in quiet anticipation.

Just then his radio crackled into life, breaking the dozy silence. It was Ben, the headman had contacted him from across the river. The poachers had arrived at his village, three truckloads, over 30 men, and they were heading down to the water's edge.

The waiting was over, he signaled all the section heads. It was definitely happening tonight.

CHAPTER 9

Night of Fire

'Oh jeez, you scared the shit out of me.' Tony jumped as Ben slipped into the hide beside him.

'Sorry... okay, not really,' Ben said mischievously, having intentionally got the jump on him. He quickly became serious. 'The pontoon boat, Vusa's, just slipped passed my hide. It didn't even attempt to stop. We should hear it shortly.'

It had been deadly quiet, with no sound except the chirruping of cicadas, the hissing of wind in the trees and occasional grunts of distant hippos. But no sooner had Ben said the words, the low roar and whine of a large outboard motor could be heard, straining as it pushed its load up against the Zambezi current.

'Here they come,' Tony half-whispered with tense anticipation. He fervently hoped this was the beach they would be pulling into. While they couldn't see much of the river through the peephole, the beat of the outboard grew louder as it rounded the downstream bend. Then its pitch changed, slowing to an idle, and through the nighttime's grey watery gloom the boat nosed into the beach. He leaned over and mouthed into Ben's ear. 'Shit, look at all of them.'

The deck of the craft, like Chinese terracotta warriors, was tightly packed with men. One jumped off the bow into the knee-high water, he trailed a rope as he ran up the beach to secure it to the trunk of a stunted flaming-red Msasa tree. As the boat's pontoons scraped onto the sandy beach, he pulled the rope taut, securing it in place.

A crush of bodies swarmed off the craft onto the beach. Initially, there was a chorus of excited chatter before a harsh word silenced the hubbub of voices.

'Silence,' a commanding voice admonished in Swahili, as its owner also exited off the bow.

'That's him, he's here,' Tony murmured, 'thank God.'

Vusa rounded on his lieutenant, Mehluki. 'Get these men in order. This isn't a Sunday School outing,' he rebuked. 'Get the gun-boys and their teams together. We move out shortly.'

He pulled the radio off his belt and spoke to the captain of the boat, instructing him to pull back into the river once the bowline was released, head down, and standoff at the mouth of the lake. He instructed him to wait there until he was radioed for the pickup after the raid.

Vusa stood watching the boat reverse back into the river and be taken away by the current. A wary feeling of déjà vu washed over him now that he was isolated on the Zimbabwean side of the Zambezi. He was taken back to those heady days as an insurgent again, he looked around, not liking what he saw. All except for his gun-boys it was like leading in new recruits again. He had to get them into cover.

He called Mehluki over. 'We will use the same game trail as before. It is well defined and easy to follow. You take the vanguard, with four men staggered back on the flanks, and I will bring up the rear with two more to cover our back-trail.' Yes, it was just like old times again, but for the Zambian porters who made up a very soft and undisciplined center. He was already starting to feel a little uneasy about this raid, but quickly brushed the thought aside. 'Move out,' he commanded.

'He is using his Matabele on the flanks and on the back-trail, we need to be very careful. Vusa himself is bringing up the rear,' Ben had come back to the hide, where Tony had been waiting impatiently for him to complete his first recce and report back. 'He is treating this like an insurgence, a military operation. He's being extremely cautious.'

'Can we follow?' was all Tony wanted to know. 'We can't afford to lose touch with them, or get too far behind.' He was thinking of his stop line, bringing it up too soon or too late would be disastrous.

'We can follow,' Ben said decisively. 'But,' he cautioned, 'you must follow my lead.'

'Yes, oh great *Bwana*,' Tony teased. 'Now go,' he ordered, never noticing the eyeroll of forbearance Ben gave as he set off after the poachers.

Initially, the lone rhino bull knew there was one man waiting above the beach, his preferred spot for drinking, and this was the man's second night of being there. He was sheltered in one of those flimsy caves that he had inspected earlier, hastily constructed and covered with vegetation. He had found a brackish puddle to drink from in the morning, so his thirst wasn't an issue. He just preferred to drink at the clean running river and didn't like these bipods invading his domain. Then he heard the scurrying sounds of another of the hated marauders come to join the first. He could hear them quietly chattering together, like a couple of nesting Guinea fowl. This only served to increase his err at having the peace of his valley intruded upon.

There was another alien manmade sound coming from down the river. It was an evasive noise, like a monotonously grumbling hippo that carried with it a stench even worse than the acrid reek of man. It was like the taint of a creosote bush, but far more pungent, now invading the sweet nighttime air.

Then unbelievably there were a multitude of these ravagers descending from what was making the sound, it looked like a small floating island, onto his beach. They seemed to be congregating below the other two, who were still hiding above them. This troubled him as it appeared they were from different herds, with the two in the cave wanting to remain hidden.

This seemed strange and he would have to think on this more, the ways of these two-legged creatures were certainly vexing. Then there was an inane jabbering, like the excited babbling of a troop of monkeys, then some sort of barked command that would emit from a dominant ape, which stopped the foreign chorus. He was now getting more agitated. He had never known this many invaders come into his home at one time.

Truly anxious now, he melted back into the bush. There would be a reckoning before this night was over. The last rhino headed to his dunghill to relieve himself, the brackish water had made his stomach rumble, he would need to be silent and mobile for what lay ahead tonight.

The progress was incredibly slow. Tony had become anxious and antsy, wishing Ben could push the pace. But he knew better than to hurry the little Matabele tracker, to do so would be at their peril. He had been squatting beside the game trail the poachers had taken. They were heading straight to the Msuna stockades, less than ten miles up near the escarpment of this section of the Zambezi Valley.

Deep in thought and distracted, he was startled when Ben snuck up beside him. 'Stop sneaking up on me like that.'

Ben ignored Tony, who was clearly agitated. 'I nearly walked into the bastards,' he whispered into his ear in breathy rasps. 'Two of Vusa's Matabele had set up on the back-trail.'

'Shit.'

'One is a smoker. I was about to round a corner and only just in time, I managed to catch a whiff of his breath. He coughed and spat, before pulling out with the other. They are leapfrogging up the game trail. I followed.' He briefly paused, catching his breath and composing himself. 'Vusa has the group in hand and is moving very slowly. He was waiting on the back-trail for these two before moving forward himself.' This clearly worried him. 'I think he senses something.'

'Voodoo superstition, he can't know anything,' Tony said with false bravado. 'Anyway, it's too late now, they are fully committed.' But he too was worried. He hoped he hadn't underestimated Vusa, but didn't want to share his concerns. The trap wouldn't be fully set until the stop line was in place.

Ben gave a disapproving cluck. 'He is a seasoned warrior. Against all odds, he lasted out the bush war. I'm telling you, Tony,' he warned, 'he may not know what's in store, but he definitely senses something.'

'Okay, point taken.' He grudgingly accepted Ben's warning. 'Now can you continue to follow?'

'Of course, in this light their spoor is clear, but the head of the poachers' column will be at the clearing below the stockades' trees, long before Vusa's rearguard. You need to warn Andy his boys have to be absolutely silent and hidden, or this will quickly turn to custard.'

As Tony radioed Andy to relay Ben's warning, he slipped away again, back up the game trail. It was clear he didn't like this one little bit. They would need to get the stop line moving soon. But he knew a body of men that size couldn't help but make some noise.

Vusa sensed more than knew. His column had stopped up ahead. He waited for his rearguard to come up to him and report. When nothing was out of order and there was no threat on their back-trail, he prepared to move forward to the main group. They would be on the edge of the clearing in front of the line of trees down from the holding stockade.

Then he heard something, and it didn't sound like any of the usual nighttime sounds of the African bush. He tensed, his unease rising as he waited, utterly still, watching and listening for the alien sound again. There it was again, something brushing through the undergrowth, but he couldn't be sure what had made the sound. It was off to his right, just off the game trail he was squatting on. He unslung the AK-47 he was carrying and disengaged the safety. He couldn't identify anything now that the clouds had covered the moon.

Then the persistent cloud cover above opened up a slither of the clear star-studded skies, exposing a glimmer of the circular moon.

The scraping noise came again. He leveled the rifle towards it, ready to pull the trigger. Then snuffling out of the undergrowth and onto the trail appeared a crested porcupine.

Vusa sighed out an anxious breath and released his grip on the trigger. The porcupine stopped warily and gazed wild-eyed at the squatting figures ahead of him. When it registered there was a threat, in fright it tensed, aggressively stamping its feet and clicking its teeth. It then rattled its quills, and like a thorny ridge they came erect forming a crest along its back.

When neither Vusa nor his men moved, it turned with quills now facing towards them. He knew the nocturnal animal was about to charge backwards and violently defend itself. He re-slung the rifle and scrambled to join the main column up the trail. His two rearguards followed him with alacrity to avoid being painfully impaled by any of its quills.

'Call in the stop line,' Ben said breathlessly, he had run back down the trail to join Tony. 'The lead line of poachers have reached the clearing. Vusa and the rearguard have closed up behind them. The clearing is their last vulnerable spot, and Vusa will take his time before committing his men out into the open.'

Tony and Ben both knew this was their chance. It appeared they would have time to get the stop line set into position.

Tony radioed his section head in charge of the stop line. Once he clipped the radio back onto his webbing, he turned back to Ben. 'We had better get back into position, or we'll be caught out here in no man's land. I'll lead, you sweep our back trail.' They hurried down a side trail, hemmed in on both sides, like impregnable walls, by thick jesse bush.

Further back down the main trail a natural depression bisected it, the 25 men of the stop line would now be moving into position along its length. Most of the rangers would be concentrated around the main trail itself. This was where they would centralize their fire. But one hundred yards either side of the trail the rest of the men would be spaced out in case some of the surviving poachers tried to make their escape through the bush. Tony and Ben would be on the far-right flank, positioned on a secondary perpendicular game trail that could offer an avenue of escape if it was discovered by any of the fleeing poachers.

They got into position and, with a now clear nighttime sky above, they had a clear field of fire in front of them. It was now time to wait for Andy to spring the trap below the stockades.

Vusa moved to the head of the column and squatted down beside Mehluki. 'Anything?' he asked, wanting to know if anything at all looked out of place.

Mehluki shook his head. 'Nothing.'

Vusa sensed there was a silent "but" that his lieutenant hadn't expressed. 'What?' he asked, he didn't want to leave anything to chance.

'I am not sure.' Mehluki was staring across the clearing, lit up by the moon like a football arena before them. 'It looks somehow different.'

'Explain,' Vusa ordered, his unease had also heightened ever since he had reached the clearing.

'The trees, their profile, somehow look different from when we were here last. I don't remember them looking like this.'

Vusa scanned the trees across the clearing, nothing looked out of the ordinary to him. He wondered if he should send a man over. Then the slither of open sky that had brought the illumination of the moon, closed, and his question was answered.

'Shit,' he swore.

It began to rain, now the trees across the clearing became a blurred watery distortion. They were starkly illuminated by a flash of lightening, but as the boom of thunder followed, Vusa's night vision was destroyed. All he saw was blackness through the driving rain. *Maybe I should call off the raid*, he thought in a moment of uncertainty. But then his greed took over. It wasn't past midnight yet, they had time.

'We need to wait for this cursed rain to clear,' he said to Mehluki, hunched beside him.

Mehluki just nodded and moved deeper into the undergrowth to take cover from the rain.

The only problem was, half an hour later it was still raining, now a steady downpour. 'Damn it,' Vusa cursed under his breath. They were now running out of time. He started calculating how much time was needed to complete the raid. He realized he would need all the remaining hours before dawn to perform it, and get the men and the booty back across the border into Zambia and on their way to Lusaka. He knew they had passed the point of no return. He either had to call off the raid and head back to the river, or give the signal to go. He hesitated a moment longer, staring anxiously into the rain, across to the blurry outline of the trees.

He looked around at the huddled mass of men around him, trying unsuccessfully to shelter against the rain. He turned to Mehluki, who with water dripping off his brow, passively waited for his decision.

Then, as the wind-driven rain lulled for a few seconds, Vusa heard the squealing trumpet of a teenage rhino mournfully calling to his mother, resonate eerily down from the stockades. That was all he needed, there was far too much profit waiting for him up there.

Without a second thought, blinded by greed, he commanded Mehluki, 'Have the gun-boys gather their porters. We move on my orders.'

He knew all his men understood what was expected of them.

Chapter 10

The Trap is Sprung

'Christ,' Tony cursed, 'I can't see a bloody thing.' He looked over at Ben, who was sheltering under a leafy wait-a-bit tree. The rain, the mosquitos, the anxiety did nothing to dim his enthusiasm. He had a grin of anticipation splashed across his sodden face. 'Bloodthirsty little bugger,' he mumbled, knowing the little man relished any type of fight, before peering back out into the rain again.

The two dozen supremely fit rangers, dressed in olive-green fatigues, had got into their positions at his stop line just before the skies opened up. But the only shelter available was from the bush around them that didn't account for much. Tony knew these men, especially after being on hard rations of dried fish and cold sadza, cooked maize meal, and living out in the open for several days with mosquitos swarming around them, were already irritated and uncomfortable. But there wasn't much he could do. The trap had already been set and within several hours this would be over, one way or the other. He thought about moving down the line and offering encouragement, but knew the ambush could be sprung at any time with an unknown number of poachers descending down upon them at any moment.

He decided he needed to stay put and let the gods of war determine how this action played out. Then he heard it, the shuddering concussion of automatic weapons fire. *Bloody finally.* The trap had been sprung, the dreaded waiting was over.

Vusa was the last to step out into the clearing. He had silently motioned Mehluki and their joint group of porters to hang back, while ordering the other gun-boys and their teams to advance, one group at a time. He judged the first group must have nearly made the far side as he and his group set off across the clearing.

They had traveled less than 20 paces when the rain-laden sky was lit up by several iridescent arcing *fusée* flares. He and Mehluki reacted, immediately going to ground, just before machine-gun and semi-automatic fire opened up from the trees on the far side of the clearing. He watched as his men, like sheaves of sickled wheat, were being cut down by rifle fire. He couldn't believe what he was seeing. This was an artful trap, and he had blundered, like a blind man, headlong into it.

'God damnit,' he snarled, but knew exactly who had set it. *That son-of-a-bitch Campbell.* He had been an idiot, but there would be time to castigate himself later. He needed to get away, to survive.

There was only one avenue of escape, and that was back the way they had come. But he sensed trouble also lay in wait in that direction too. He looked around frantically. He needed a distraction. Milling around him his group of Zambian porters were still on their feet, but quickly realizing they were in danger, seeing their colleagues shot and falling down in front of them. He knew it wouldn't take much to send them into frantic headlong flight.

'Back to the trees, head to the river. Run,' he yelled, 'run for your lives!'

Without waiting to be told again, the porters turned and, like spooked scrub hares, began with reckless haste to run. And Vusa now had his distraction, the porters would take the brunt of whatever waited further down the trail.

He noticed Mehluki hadn't moved and was laying with his AK-47 leveled towards the trees ahead, defending their position. 'Good man,' he mumbled, acknowledging his lieutenant's defensive nous. Also, miraculously, it appeared two other gun-boys had survived the ambush. The rain and poor visibility had obviously aided their retreat. One dove to ground beside him, the other beside Mehluki. Several other porters ran to their position, but didn't stop as they scrambled in wide-eyed terror back the way they had come.

Vusa realized the three men laying concealed around him were waiting for orders. At a time like this it felt good to have real men under his command. He knew he could use them to his best advantage. He also knew the ambushers up ahead would soon set up skirmish lines and would be coming down to meet them. It was time to get back into the trees before they were caught out in the open.

'Back to the edge of the clearing,' he ordered, from there he would plan their retreat. He was already thinking like a soldier again, knowing he needed to perform a tactical retreat.

As they got under cover, with rifle at the ready, Vusa realized it had stopped raining and the clouds above were starting to dissipate. A watery pale-yellow moon starkly illuminated the ground around them.

As Vusa assessed their situation, automatic weapons fire erupted further down the back-trail behind them, the fleeing porters being cut down one by one.

He had attackers in front and now behind, soon they will also perform a pincer movement, closing off the sides. He was effectively trapped. But through all his years of war, he had never been bested by any man. He had always survived, and while the situation appeared hopeless he was sure tonight would be no different. Now it was time to somehow figure out how to get away.

It was Mehluki who gave him the only viable option. 'There is a side trail that branches off the main one. It is not too far away. You sent me down it the last time we were here. It meets the main trail closer to the river.'

Through the nighttime gloom, Vusa stared at his lieutenant in confusion. Then like a lifer miraculously being offered parole, realization hit. He remembered the entrance to the side trail and knew he had a chance to escape what Campbell had obviously crafted as well-laid plans.

Tony heard the rattling fire of automatics centralized around where the main trail intersected the stop line. He was surprised at the volume and length of the salvos, a lot more poachers must have escaped the ambush up at the stockades. He would have loved to know if Vusa had been a casualty there or in the clearing below the trees. But he maintained radio silence waiting until he knew Andy's skirmish lines had cleared the ground down to the bottom of the clearing. Until then he would sit tight and cover the possibility of any poachers using the side trail in front of him. At least now he could see again, with the open sky and the shining moon, radiating a muted but luminescent view. After the rain it seemed the nighttime gloom had been washed away.

There was another series of shuddering reports, but this time located among the bush closer to his position. *A second wave of escapees,* he decided, not wanting to run headlong into the same fate as their colleagues on the trail. Instead they had tried a direct route to escape through the bush but obviously met with the same demise.

'That's probably the last of them,' Tony hazarded.

'No,' Ben contradicted, 'I believe Vusa is still out there. We haven't heard any return fire at all, especially the repetitive clack of an AK-47.'

Tony realized that was true. So far it had been all one-way traffic, none of his carefully laid positions had come under fire. He knew with Vusa and his group of trained Matabele, they should have heard that distinctive sound. 'You're right,' Tony agreed. 'Unless someone scored a lucky hit. But yes, he'll still probably be out there and will have his remaining men well in hand.'

Bugger, Tony knew this mission was far from over.

There was another shuddering blast of automatic fire, the second wave of porters getting culled. *They are unimportant*, Vusa ignored what was happening to them. It was time to move.

'You know this trail, you will lead,' he said to Mehluki, then he organized the other two gun-boys to be on the flanks, while he would bring up the rear. 'Go,' he ordered his lieutenant, but quickly cautioned, 'be wary that this trail isn't also a trap.'

Mehluki didn't run on the trail. He moved steadily, scanning for any sign of manmade disturbance. It was difficult going as the bush hemmed in their progress on both sides, reducing them to single file at times. They were coming up to a corner and Mehluki stepped into a slight recess in the close-knit bush before getting too close to it. He waited for Vusa to join him.

'I have seen no sign of any kind, or anything indicating an ambush,' he said in a hoarse whisper. 'But around the bend is a natural depression, an ideal place for one.' He paused, visualizing what he had described. 'The depression also runs sideways to the main trail and dissects it. It is roughly in line with the shots we heard earlier. If there is an ambush, it will be there.'

Vusa knew if Campbell were anywhere, he would be just around the corner, like a black mamba silently waiting to attack. He looked at the bush either side of the trail. It looked impregnable, there would be no way to easily bypass this position without signaling their presence, no matter how stealthy they tried to be.

'How far around the bend would they be waiting?' he whispered, trying to formulate a plan.

'Twenty paces,' Mehluki whispered back with certainty.

'And the bush either side of the trail?' Vusa wanted to know what cover was available to them.

'Like this. We will be exposed all the way.'

'A direct approach is our only option.' Vusa looked at his men, calculating the odds. He would lose at least two of them. Acceptable, he decided. 'If they are there, they will not be expecting us, and we will be on top of them before they know it,' he tried to soften the death sentence he was about to pass.

With complete trust, they seemed to accept the lie.

He looked at Mehluki. *Well, maybe not him*, he realized. He indicated the two other gun-boys. 'You two will lead, you will be the sharpened point of my *assegai*, my spear, that will be thrust into the heart of the enemy. We will cover you.'

One of them puffed out his chest eagerly. *He will probably be the first to die*, Vusa knew. 'You go hard and fast, but only shoot if there is trouble. Stop when you reach the next defensible position.' He looked at Mehluki, who nodded, accepting that these men were as good as dead to them. He was ready.

'Go,' Vusa ordered, and watched briefly as the two men leapt up and ran at their best speed for the bend, before they followed them. Of course he was securely protected at the rear of the group.

Tony was starting to believe his plan had been a resounding success. He knew Andy's skirmish lines would already be at the bottom edge of the clearing. There had been no more disruption of gunfire, nor any indication that his men had met with resistance. He was starting to relax, thinking through the raft of post-action requirements to mop up the mission.

It was the harsh rattling bark of Ben's FN beside him that made him jump, jolting him back to the here and now.

'Oh shit!' With his heart thumping wildly, he saw there were two armed men coming headlong straight towards their position. *No, there were more*, he could see, *running behind, sprinting down upon them.*

Time seemed to slow down. He saw Ben's raking shots hit the first man. One in the groin, the second in the guts and the third squarely in the center of his chest.

The next man was perhaps ten paces away from him, like an Olympic athlete he hurdled his fallen comrade and before his legs had hit the ground, was firing from the hip.

Ben ducked to his side as several bullets welted into the ground, kicking up dirt, where he would have been. Tony brought up his rifle and pointed it up towards the rapidly closing figure. He snapped off a reflex shot. It was a fluke and caught the man in the throat, killing him instantly. The man immediately stopped firing but his momentum, with blood gushing like a ruptured water main, carried him forward to tumble with arms and rifle flaying in between where Tony and Ben were positioned. Tony had to jump aside, but the man's rifle still hit him, a glancing blow across his temple. He was briefly stunned as two more men barged through their position, they didn't fire a shot, intent only in their escape.

With scant regard for the dead, the last man stomped squarely on his fallen comrade's chest as he ran through the depression.

Tony would have recognized him anywhere. It was Vusa, but he was too stunned to do a thing about it.

Ben was recovering quickly. He swung his rifle on the fleeing men and just before they rounded the next bend in the trail, let off a long raking burst. He thought he saw the first man hunch his shoulders as he rounded out of sight, but couldn't be sure. He would have followed but saw Tony was in difficulty beside the man he had shot.

'Are you hit?' he called out with concern, the two fleeing poachers temporarily forgotten.

'Ah, no... the AK,' Tony pointed to it on the ground, 'caught me on the head. Gimme a minute, I'll be fine.'

'Give me your radio,' Ben demanded briskly, now disregarding Tony's injuries, 'that was Vusa and Mehluki. We need to cut them off before they reach the river.'

Holding his head, Tony handed over his radio. He listened, struggling to his feet, as Ben ordered the section head commanding the stop line to take half his men and set up again at the junction where the side trail joined the main one. He also radioed the two rangers manning the upriver hides to position themselves in cover, above the landing beach, in case Vusa got through before the new stop line was in place. He handed the radio back to Tony.

'We need to get after them, but of course only after you've finished lounging around,' he mocked good-naturedly, stepping in to look at Tony's head.

'Bugger off,' he said impatiently, slapping his hand away. 'Go, I'll be fine.'

Ben, with Tony staggering behind, set off down the trail.

Neither Vusa nor Mehluki slowed down as they ran through the ambush site. They saw both men running in front of them go down, dead or mortally wounded. They were of no concern and had served their purpose.

But Vusa had recognized Tony, now regretting he hadn't fired at the man. As they were about to round the first corner, Vusa flinched and ducked his head, his hated enemy forgotten as all around him, like a whiplash of angry wasps, a fuselage of bullets zipped about his head. He noticed Mehluki stagger slightly, obviously hit, but then seemed to steady himself and run on.

It wasn't until they had run about a mile that Vusa noticed a large dark patch had slowly spread across Mehluki's T-shirt and his pace began to falter.

'Damn it,' Vusa cursed to himself. Mehluki getting injured was incredibly inconvenient. Until he was across the river Vusa needed him fighting fit, after that he didn't care whether the man lived or died. He saw an open patch of scrub up ahead. 'Wait up, I will tend your shoulder,' he ordered reluctantly.

When they stopped Vusa pulled up his lieutenant's shirt. The wound was high up on the shoulder, a through-and-through wound.

'It is a little thing,' Mehluki said, neither wincing nor grunting as Vusa palpated the wound. But he could see the man must have been in pain, even in the softened nighttime light his pallor had lost its luster and taken on a grayish sheen.

'You will live,' Vusa grunted, and he was telling the truth. 'It is only a flesh wound. Tomorrow, it will have stiffened up and you will have lost the use of the arm. You may be in pain, but tonight you will be able to fight.'

'As I said, it is a little thing,' and to a seasoned warrior like Mehluki it was. He had experienced far worse during the war.

Vusa dropped his T-shirt. 'Where are we?'

'We are about 12 klicks,' he used the military term for kilometers, 'from the beach. But we are about ten from where this trail meets the main one, where they will be waiting for us again.'

Yes, that bastard Campbell has us hemmed in, Vusa knew, *and would also be coming up behind.* 'How can we avoid Campbell and his *izimpungushe*, his jackals?' He felt sure Mehluki would have at least one more trick up his sleeve.

'There is a hidden pathway, halfway between here and the beach,' he explained, 'it will be hard going, but it will take us to the river. It goes through–'

'Go, take us there,' Vusa briskly cut him off. He didn't care what it went through just as long as it got them out of here.

Once he was sure, without stopping, Ben quietly relayed to Tony what he read in the spoor. 'We are perhaps five, ten minutes behind them. One is wounded. I'm pretty sure it's Mehluki, but it doesn't seem to have slowed him down too much. He is still leading and... DOWN, DOWN, DOWN!' he screamed urgently, as he dove for cover, with Tony instantly following suit.

They had both taken evasive action and gone to ground, rolling over several times to throw off anyone's aim, and brought their rifles up at the ready. After a couple of minutes, when no shots were fired at them, they came to their feet warily.

Ben went back to the track, looking down and around at the ground.

'What?' Tony demanded, now fully recovered. He was still smarting after taking the knock to the head, letting Vusa brazenly run through their position, and now having to dive for cover for apparently nothing.

'They have left the trail, stay where you are,' Ben ordered. He didn't want Tony confusing the sign. He backtracked and grunted with reluctant admiration at the anti-tracking the men they were following had performed.

For about 200 paces back up the trail Vusa and Mehluki had walked carefully backwards in their own prints before stepping lightly off the track and onto a well-concealed pathway. Any vegetation and grass that had been damaged as they stepped from the trail had been deftly straightened and put back into place. It was the stalk of tufty elephant grass that hinged back over at the spot it was originally damaged that caught Ben's attention to where they had exited.

'Huh,' Ben grunted with grudging recognition at the skill with which the anti-tracking had been performed. 'They left the trail here. They are now following the lesser trails.' But he felt if it had been during daylight hours, not during the muted wash of the harvest moon, he would never have missed this ruse.

'How far behind are we?' Tony wanted to know, becoming impatient.

'As I said, it could be five or ten minutes. But now they are amongst the jesse it could only be a minute, if they are waiting for us—'

'Which they probably are,' Tony finished for Ben.

They both knew if they couldn't hear them fighting through this tangle of undergrowth, it meant they had set up an ambush of their own.

What the hell to do? Tony mused. *Wait until daylight and bring in all my men, or go in now and try and flush them out?* But he knew with someone of Vusa's caliber, he could easily slip past any cordon he set up. He had to go in now or lose the murderous bastard for good.

'Take the spoor,' he commanded, knowing they were walking into a trap as, like a hangman's noose, the bush closed in around them.

CHAPTER 11

The Showdown

THE STENCH, LIKE a solid thing, stopped both men in their tracks. It was a rank gamey smell, like a cattle pen but far more pungent. It was incredibly invasive and overpowering, and like a clinging mist, the air only moved reluctantly as they forged their way deeper into the small densely-walled clearing. Strewn about them was a massive dung heap of digested bark, twigs and vegetation, where a rhino returned daily to defecate.

'It is a rhino's midden,' Mehluki said over his shoulder to Vusa, who huddled in the bush behind him in anticipation.

What neither man realized was that the dunghill had only recently been used.

'Campbell is following.' Vusa's gut told him. 'We will wait for him here. The smell will hopefully distract him.' He knew if he could cull Campbell, the chase would falter, and he would have a better than even chance of getting away. He looked at Mehluki. 'We will set a trail as if we walked through this stinking place, but,' he pointed to the far side of the clearing, 'we will set up over there, in clear view of where they will enter.'

It took the men five tense minutes of anti-tracking to set up the ambush. And once they were in position, they could hear their pursuit pushing their way through the jesse bush, about to enter their prepared killing zone.

'Just one clear shot,' Vusa whispered desperately, as he lined up his AK-47 on the false trail they had made along the edge of the dunghill. The small clearing was open to the nighttime sky, its eerie illuminance bathing it in a kaleidoscope of varying monochrome light.

Ben stopped in his tracks. It was the nauseating smell that did it. 'A midden,' he whispered back to Tony, now this trail made sense to him, rhinos always liked to do their business in private. He was about to step forward when Tony stopped him.

'Wait!' Tony grabbed his shoulder. 'How far behind are we?'

'Five minutes, maybe a couple more,' Ben calculated from the look of the spoor he had been following.

'Are we closing on them?'

'Yes, definitely. In this thick bush, we should just about be able to hear them, or at least those creatures they disturb.'

'But we haven't,' Tony said insistently. 'Not one whistle from a nightjar, or a startled bushbuck crashing through the jesse. It's deathly silent.'

Ben then realized it too. He should have noticed. He had been too intent on the spoor and the rank lingering odor had distracted him. Now ignoring the smell, he looked warily at the entrance to the clearing, following the line of spoor. It now looked too distinctive.

'Yes, they are in there waiting.' He looked back at Tony and could see he had figured it out before him.

Tony realized they couldn't stealthily navigate around the midden, their progress would be heard. Their only safe avenue was back the way they came, or they could wait. He knew it would be suicide stepping into the clearing. He decided to wait it out and whispered as such to Ben.

A tense and torturous hour crawled by as Tony began to wonder if Vusa had found another well-defined pathway on the other side of the dunghill and was now making his escape across the river. Then he heard the alarm cry of an oxpecker.

'That was weird,' he wondered aloud. Normally these little red or yellow-billed birds that rode on the backs of large mammals to eat the pesky bugs and ticks, preferred open ground, and were only present in thick bush when perched on a host.

'Something disturbed the *Askari wa kifaru*,' Ben whispered to Tony, giving the oxpecker the Swahili name for the rhino's guard.

'But it wasn't us, it came from the other side of the clearing,' Tony reasoned, but neglected to understand the importance of the bird actually being present.

'They are over there,' Ben pointed with his chin through the entry to the other side of the clearing. 'The waiting is getting to them. They are restless and disturbed the bird.' Ben, too, failed to understand the importance of the bird.

'They may be pulling out. If there is any more noise, we move,' Tony instructed, readying himself for action.

Vusa jumped with fright when the oxpecker cried out. With animal cunning he hadn't moved and was completely focused on where Campbell would enter the clearing, since staking out the ambush. But with Mehluki it was another matter entirely. His shoulder was starting to stiffen and with each insistent throb of his heart the wound, like a sledge hammer, pounded with pain. He had to move, the agony had become like a living, gnawing thing. He had tried to round the shoulder to relieve the torture, but it had been a clumsy effort and his arm had spasmed, causing him to scrape it across the ground while he suppressed a grunt of pain. It was this that had alarmed the bird.

'Quiet, you idiot,' Vusa spat at his lieutenant, looking at him in aghast astonishment.

But Mehluki couldn't help it. His shoulder began to severely spasm and cramp, and he had to bury his face in the crook of his other arm as he rode wave after wave, like the swells of a storm-strewn sea, of gut-wrenching anguish. He tried to suppress his breathing, but he couldn't prevent it from coming out as stifled groans. He was incapacitated.

From the noise Mehluki was making, there was another explosive cry of oxpeckers, with them now bursting into flight, from somewhere close behind the two men.

Then all hell broke loose and Vusa wasn't ready for the storm of bullets and the two attackers behind the fuselage running straight at them from across the clearing.

Tired of the waiting, Tony was the first to move. He didn't aim he just approximated his charge by the raucous cries of the oxpeckers. He went straight up and over the dung heap, saw movement in front of him, and kept running and firing straight towards it. Ben followed closely off to his side doing the same.

Tony was running down the other side of the mount of dung when one of his legs found a hole, caught, and he tripped just as a barrage of bullets opened fire. They harmlessly flew over the top of him. He rolled when he hit the bottom of the heap, leapt back up and then crashed in on top of the man firing his weapon, just past the edge of the clearing. Their rifles were now useless, it was hand-to-hand combat.

Tony recognized him instantly. 'Vusa,' he hissed as he went to work.

Ben was just behind Tony, and saw him go down and bound back up. He was screaming as he ran and fired, caught up in the berserker's rage that carried him forward. He saw Tony smash into one of the two men waiting in ambush, and the other man was now up on his knees trying to awkwardly level an AK-47 up at him. As he got closer, he saw the scar and realized it was Mehluki. Before his opponent was able to bring his rifle to bear, he too was on top of him. The kneeing, punching and elbows began.

The rhino didn't understand what was going on. He watched the whirl of snatching hands, stomping feet, angry shouts, his rounded tulip-shaped ears twitching back and forth.

These men, these invaders, seemed to be trying to kill one another.

Earlier he had just finished his business after hearing the burst of barking thunderous shouts that always seemed to accompany these odd two-legged creatures, reverberating way off in the distance. He was about to go in search of these marauders, when suddenly he realized he didn't need to, they were coming to him. He could hear men moving, like a troop of baboons on a foraging party, clumsily making their way through the bush towards him, to his private place.

Stealthily, making no sound for such a large animal, he moved from the clearing and stood back among the jesse bush on the far side of the clearing, well away from where they would enter.

Two men stepped into the clearing, walked around it, then unbelievably crept to hide in the bush just off to the side, in front of him. They appeared to be looking back the way they had come, as if laying like hunting leopards, waiting for something. While he could smell their acrid scent, he knew his dung masked his smell and made him invisible to them. Incensed that they had intruded not just into his valley but now into his hidden intimate place, he was about to move and vent his rage on this hated enemy. Then he heard another clumsy approach, more men were coming from the same direction as these other two, but they never stepped into the clearing. They had stopped and were waiting, concealed, on the other side of the entrance. He wondered what they were doing. In his mind, he positioned both sets of men. He stood stock-still, waiting to see what happened. The ways of these disgusting invasive creatures was strange.

As the moon passed through its nighttime arch, he knew it was getting closer to dawn. The colorless light hadn't yet strengthened, but twisting a tulip-shaped ear backwards he heard the fluttering wings of several oxpeckers coming in to land on his rump. Dawn was approaching, these sentinels had risen and were out looking for their first morning's meal. He grudgingly accepted their presence, ignoring them.

He flicked his ears forward, concentrating back on these quietly waiting men, trying to figure out what was happening. One man in front of him grunted and moved erratically, causing a squawk from one of the birds on his back.

Then after a brief silence the same man, emitted what sounded like the snuffling snorts of a warthog, sending the oxpeckers into raucous flight. Almost simultaneously, the two men across the clearing came yelling and screaming like demented monkeys across his dung heap. They were accompanied by those rattling barking instruments that bellowed thunder and fire.

Stunned at the noise and the men's disconcerting actions, the rhino was about to turn and flee. But then he realized none of this was directed at him. The loud noises and running had stopped, and these men were now fighting chest to chest, but for what, territory? Maybe they were after his private place? But now there was a huge scuffle going on right in front of him. With so much movement, he could clearly place the brawl. They were tearing at each other like warring baboons.

Should I leave and let these two-legged apes fight it out and destroy each other? he questioned, *or should I help them achieve their goal?*

Vusa let go of his rifle as Campbell collided into him. He needed his hands for what he knew lay ahead. He punched and kneed his hated opponent, operating purely on instinct. But then he was shocked to realize they were no longer matched, not like they had been when they first confronted one another during the war. In addition to being older than Campbell, he was no longer an insurgent, a finely-tuned fighting machine. The easy years of living in the flesh pot of Lusaka, from the wealth and privilege he had created from the spoils of poaching had made him soft. Here he was fighting a man hardened from years of pursuing poachers and roughing it in the bush as a game ranger. But still he grimly fought on.

Tony was insanely angry. The rage that he carried for Vusa, his orchestrated poaching and his previous attack, boiled over as he went for him. The barbaric slaughter of innocent creatures and his friends and coworkers in that gruesome raid was seared into his memory. He wanted to kill this man for all that he had done, tear his limbs off with his bare hands. He struck out with all the weapons at his disposal, hands and feet, elbows and knees, and he could feel he was beating down and overpowering this vile mercenary. He struck and punched, easily evading what Vusa threw at him. He had swung a backhanded chop with the blade of his hand at his throat. It hit with only a glancing strike as Vusa leant backwards to avoid the blow. Then, knowing he had the upper hand and would soon overwhelm him, Tony made the near-fatal mistake of glancing over and checking on Ben, who was engaged in a fierce battle of his own, but with an opponent much larger than him.

Seeing Campbell was distracted, Vusa took his chance. Like a striking adder, he drew his head back even further, then butted savagely forward with all his might and smashed into an eye and the bridge of his nose.

Stunned and seeing stars, Tony staggered backwards with a gush of blood pouring out of his nose. The blow had also cut his eyebrow to the bone, with a flap of skin now hanging down blinding him in that eye. With tears pouring from the other one, due to the broken nose, he was immobilized. A roundhouse punch from Vusa to the side of his head sent him lurching to the ground.

Vusa quickly scooped up his AK-47. He could see Campbell was out of action, at least for now, but he could also see Mehluki was making heavy going against the vicious little terrier of a man attacking him. He felt like shooting Mehluki, along with Campbell's little Matabele, for what his lieutenant had just brought down upon them, but reasoned he would probably need the stupid bastard before the night was out. He put a three-bullet-tap into the ground at their feet. Shocked, both men immediately stopped fighting, looking startled over at him.

Vusa signaled Ben to get over with Campbell. 'Help him up,' he shouted, 'I want him standing when I kill him.'

Ben helped Tony up off the ground, who was shaking his head trying to clear his muddled brain.

'As I told you once before, Campbell, you are the vanquished. You were then and you certainly are now. But I must say your trap was artfully laid. It nearly worked.'

Tony was slowly recovering, at least he could see out of one eye now. 'Screw you, Vusa.'

'I think not, Campbell. It appears you're the one that is screwed. You may have wiped out most of my gang, but I'll rebuild it. But for that little inconvenience...' He paused, trailing off. 'Well, I think you know what's about to happen.'

Tony felt like a wounded and cornered animal. He knew he was about to die and that Vusa would rebuild. Without capturing or killing him, he knew he had gained little. He had hoped to give the rhinos in this valley some respite. Sure, the ones up in the stockade would be relocated after they had foiled this attack, but with a man like Vusa still controlling the poaching on this side of the Zambezi, the black rhino in this region were as good as extinct. For that alone Tony felt a sudden bitter regret.

It was Ben who reacted first as Vusa brought up the rifle ready to pull the trigger. He quickly sucked in a fearful breath, but not from what Vusa was about to do.

Something compelled the rhino to stay. He was on the verge of leaving these strange creatures to their fate, but as the scuffle quietened down and appeared to turn into a standoff, he stealthily walked forward. The closer he came to the man who now seemed to be the prevailing alpha male, the more malevolently evil he sensed him and the one beside him were. These invaders had somehow brought death to his valley, and while he had always thought all men were the same, these other two seemed to be trying to stop them. This seemed very odd to him.

Without a sound the bull came rocketing out of the bush, intent on destroying the evil that emanated from the one in front of him.

The first Tony knew that Vusa was incapacitated was when a sharp, rapier-like rhino horn exited through the front of his chest. It had gone through him like a hot knife through butter.

Impaled, Vusa hung briefly in the air. With his mouth gaping, opening and closing, like a stranded fish, and with his eyes bulging out in shocked amazement. His arms went limp and the rifle dropped. He stared down in disbelief at the blood-stained horn sticking out from his chest, but slowly the sheen of life faded from his eyes.

With what seemed like a casual flick, the rhino cast Vusa's body aside. He then pivoted slightly, hooking to his side. He caught Mehluki just above his hip, with the horn driving through his flank, up through the rib cage and ripping through skin as if it were tissue paper. Mehluki was screaming as he was brutally shaken off the horn. The screaming abruptly stopped when the rhino stepped forward, placed his foot on the wailing man's chest and crushed it into a pulp.

Hearts racing, eyes gaping in the strengthening twilight, Tony and Ben stood perfectly still, staring at the rhino. Neither of them had ever heard of a rhino soundlessly stealing forward and casually perform such acts of violence. Something that almost never happened. This rhino had acted like a cold and calculating hunter.

The rhino stared short-sightedly at them both. He knew they were there and they knew that he knew it. Like statues cast in stone, neither man moved for if they did they knew they would have met a similar fate as Vusa and Mehluki.

The beast paused, as if considering what to do with them. He just stood there owlishly peering at them through his long-curved lashes. Eventually, with his mind made up, he snorted once blowing a misty cloud of blood from around his nostrils.

He sensed these two were no danger and would leave them. He stamped the ground and trotted off. He had a valley to patrol and protect.

EPILOGUE

Loose Ends

TONY WAS SILENT as Ben tendered to his wounds. He had taken a field dressing from his webbing and was hastily patching up the flap of skin that hung over his injured eye. 'Obviously you'll need to get it stitched.' As he was cleaning up his wounds, he noticed his nose was crooked. 'He sucker punched you. I thought you would have had him easily.'

'I was, but then did something stupid,' he said sarcastically, shifting the blame. 'A constant failing of mine, something I'm continually forced to do. I looked over at your sorry arse to make sure you were alright.'

'Archangel Tony? Don't think so. I can take care of myself,' Ben said, grabbing his crooked nose.

'Yeah right, you…' Tony trailed off and howled in agony, a gush of tears streaming down his cheeks. Ben had deftly twisted and yanked the nose straight again. '*Oww!* That hurts like a motherfucker.'

'Such a cry baby.' Ben admonished. 'Should have left it hooked to the side, would've improved your looks.'

Tony was swearing on the side of the dung heap, stamping his feet with his hands cupped over his face. 'You bastard, motherless prick, son-of-a-bitch, born from a two-timing whore.'

'Make up your mind, I either have a mother or I don't. Christ, you do go on.'

But Tony wasn't listening.

Leaving him swearing, Ben left him and walked to the two bodies on the edge of the clearing. He briefly searched them. As he suspected, they carried no identification. He then walked around the perimeter of the clearing and off in the direction the rhino had taken.

Within five minutes Ben was back again. He stood over Tony, who was still blinking his eyes rapidly trying to clear the tears of agony. 'I know who our savior was.'

'Savior?' Tony blinked blankly up at him, still getting over having his nose so unceremoniously straightened.

'Who it was that saved us... the rhino.'

'How so?' Tony was clearly bemused, still in awe of what he had witnessed.

'It's the rhino we've been tracking. The last rhino in the corridor. I recognized his prints.'

'No shit.' Tony forgot about his nose as he rose, brushing dried dung and vegetation off the seat of his pants. 'Well, I'll be... I knew he was an impressive animal, but to take down a poaching ring is quite something.'

'Good to see the animals fighting back.'

Tony looked over at the gory heap of the two dead men. 'Well deserved.' He couldn't have imagined a better ending than this marvel of a creature who so definitively dispatched the men likely responsible for the massacre of his family.

As they trekked back to the river, Tony had a lot to occupy his mind.

After Vusa's foiled raid, ZimParks laid an official complaint with the Zimbabwe Republic Police. The police issued an arrest warrant for Jacob Vusa, Zimbabwean citizen, whose whereabouts were currently unknown. The warrant was forwarded to the magistrates court in Kariba, a summons for his arrest, and criminal and civil cases against him were duly processed. Once the paperwork was in place, Tony requested a meeting with the magistrate, Edward Makomo, in chambers.

Tony looked like he had just gone 12 rounds with Muhammad Ali, his nose badly swollen, with a black eye and neat row of black stitches evident across his eyebrow. He came straight to the point of his requested meeting.

'We are asking under the Parks and Wild Life Act that Jacob Vusa be charged in absence for the crime of poaching a specially protected species.'

'And this Jacob Vusa is the person we discussed recently?' the magistrate asked, trying his best to ignore Tony's battered state.

'Yes, two nights ago a raiding party of 36 Zambian poachers, led by him, crossed the Zambezi.' They had counted all the dead gun-boys and porters, so Tony knew the number was accurate. 'The attack was focused on the rhinos held at the ZimParks holding stockades at Msuna. Most of his men were killed during the defense of the stockades, but Vusa and one of his henchmen escaped into the bush.'

Makomo leant forward with elbows on his desk, steepling his fingers. 'And your injuries? They were also caused by him?'

'Ah... yes, not one of my proudest moments.'

'So, we will add criminal assault to a ZimParks official,' the magistrate said decisively. 'But his whereabouts are currently unknown?'

'Correct,' Tony didn't hesitate with his answer. And it was true, more or less. Where exactly he ended up he couldn't accurately say.

Makomo fell silent and clasped his fingers over his ample belly. 'Herein lies the problem. Even if the act is *actus reus*,' he used the Latin, 'an act which is illegal, we must still follow the due process of the law. Even if Vusa was *deprensis*, caught in the act, so to speak, which it appears he was, as the state of your personage due to his attempted apprehension will attest, we still must presume he's innocent until proven otherwise in a court of law.'

'But can't we conduct a hearing, appoint a defense and still try him in absence?' Tony wanted to know.

'In *absentia*? Effectively, no. As both criminal and civil laws were alleged to be broken, cases against the defendant must, firstly be duly entered with the court, and according to the Criminal Procedures and Evidence Act when a suspect is out of custody, this falls into sections 130 through 142 of the act,' Makomo recited from memory. 'A summons must be issued for either his appearance, or a warrant for his arrest. Which I understand the latter in this case has been done. In fact, I know this to be true, as I signed the originating writ. But,' he got back on track with his explanation, 'for either of these to be effective there has to be an actual arrest, so the defendant, in this case Vusa, can appear and answer the charges laid before him. However,' he untwined his fingers and shook one in warning, 'if the summons or warrant hasn't been acknowledged or processed, as laid down in section 160, if the defendant is not brought to trial after the expiration of six months from the date of his committal for trial, the cases must be dismissed. This is also supported by caselaw in the matter of *Mukuze and Anor vs The Attorney General.*'

Tony stared at him, incredulously. 'So the charges are dropped, and he gets off scot-free for murdering the rangers and thousands of animals?'

'Good lord, no,' Makomo was horrified at such an assumed miscarriage of justice. 'The charges remain *adjourned sine die*, they remain for perpetuity. Effectively they can be brought against him at any time in the future. Once the man has been arrested he can be tried accordingly. Other than this, it is *ultra vires*, beyond my control.'

And therein lies the problem, Tony thought bitterly, *it's impossible.* Only he and Ben knew Vusa would never be able to be brought to trial. He had hoped charges and a fine could be levied against the man, with an official request being brought through diplomatic channels so the proceeds from the sale of Vusa's Zimbabwean and Zambian assets could be supplied to ZimParks for their much-needed fight against poaching. He tried another angle. 'So… could there be extenuating circumstances?' Makomo nodded thoughtfully, but remained silent as he let Tony finish. 'What if Vusa died while in the bush, and if by some miracle, his remains were discovered, would their positive identification help us gain restitution?'

Makomo was silent for many minutes contemplating what Tony had said. He was clearly searching through his vast legal memory banks for a judicial precedent for this type of circumstance.

'Possibly,' he hedged warily. He obviously hadn't thought that far ahead, but was quickly catching up with Tony's logic. He composed himself, preparing his explanation. 'If this Vusa was a ZIPRA freedom fighter as you say, then he will be classed as a war hero with *ex post facto*, retroactive, medical, dental and service records entered with the army after independence, and under an obscure and little-known act, the National Museums and Monuments of Zimbabwe Act, in conjunction with the government's Fallen Heroes Trust, if any remains recovered are positively identified as belonging to those who fought in the War of Liberation, then that positive identification can be used to substantiate a claim of restitution.' He puffed himself up, readying himself to deliver what he obviously considered the *coup de grâce*. He shook his finger, again to emphasize his point. 'Also, if I am not mistaken, caselaw, *ZIPRA vs Fallen Heroes Trust*, will support this. In fact,' he ended decisively, 'I am certain of it.'

After Makomo's long-winded explanation, Tony left the magistrate's chambers fuming, thinking there were plenty of laws but not much bloody enforcement. Under the circumstances, he knew identification would be remote. Vusa's body was probably long gone, devoured by scavengers. He accepted he would have to be content with putting Vusa out of business permanently, bringing down a big poaching syndicate, and restoring peace to the Zambezi Valley. But he decided, just to put the matter to rest and make sure, he would send out a patrol to see what they could find.

He also realized once the news got back to Lusaka that Vusa had disappeared, and his silent partnership payments, or more correctly bribes, weren't paid, it wouldn't take long before those greedy government officials and politicians, and probably some of his own employees, redistributed his assets accordingly.

Shalan bin Yehaye Hbubari always looked after number one. Ever since he began working for Vusa he had taken what he considered an acceptable payment, over and above the remuneration he had negotiated for his employment.

Soon after arriving in Lusaka, it had only taken him a few weeks to recruit one of the warehouse security guards into his pay. The guard turned a blind eye to anything hidden into a secret round compartment within the middle of his prayer matt that he brought and removed each day from work. The man accepted what Hbubari considered a pittance for looking the other way. Not once had he come close to being caught. Vusa may have understood the value of his goods, but he had no clue of the acceptable wastage during the manufacturing process.

Hbubari was powdering all the offcuts and bench findings, but the weights never took into consideration the ballast added within the handle to aid in the balance of the blades. This ballast accounted for a considerable percentage of horn that Hbubari was able to appropriate for his own personal use.

He had also hired one of the Kunda ironsmiths to make him his very own blades. He found it strange that Vusa never took inventory of any of these, which would have assisted him in accurately determining the true weight of horn being used for the handles. Already Hbubari had many finished *thuma*, with their distinctive round knobs and his own gold coins on their handles. All these blades were housed in their unique *thusa* sheaths. He had no qualms taking what he thought was fair and just, as he believed it was his right under Allah.

As soon as Hbubari heard the whisperings that Vusa's gun-boys and porters were killed, with him and his lieutenant missing, he waited one more day before snapping into action. He knew once his employer's disappearance became common knowledge, the officials he paid off would all come sweeping in like vultures and strip the place bare. For two days, he stayed in the warehouse all night, cleaning house, removing all unprocessed horn, handles and blades in production, and finished products. Exhausted but ecstatic, he paid Douglas Tanaka to truck all of this to the humble residence he kept in the school-friendly suburb of Makeni, in the west of Lusaka.

Hbubari was now an exceedingly wealthy man. All he had to do was evade Vusa's silent partners clamoring for his produce and get it safely to Yemen. He would need to pray on this. Though it was an hour short of the noon day hour, he immediately went for his prayer matt.

The morning after moving the stolen contraband for Hbubari, Douglas

Tanaka was arrested when he showed up for work at Mana Pools. The police took him for questioning. When they told him he was in serious trouble, he stammered, 'But… I haven't done anything wrong.' At first he insisted he had nothing to do with any poaching raids and denied even knowing Jacob Vusa. They coerced and threatened that he'd rot in prison if he didn't tell them what he knew, but the old Shona steadfastly held his ground.

Two officers had him in a starkly lit interrogation room at Kariba's Police Station just off Nyamhunga Drive. There were no windows, one bright single bulb overhead, and only a solid-metal panel door at the entrance of the room. They had been interrogating him for several hours with little success when a knock at the paneled door interrupted their questioning. One of the officers got up and opened it a crack. After a few quiet words, the door was opened fully and in walked a large well-built white man, with a terribly bruised and battered face, accompanied by a diminutive black man, both wearing ZimParks ranger uniforms.

All color drained from Tanaka's face. He shrunk down in his seat as both men sat across the table from him. Neither man said a word as they quietly stared across at him for a few long, torturous minutes.

Tanaka didn't know what was worse, the sight of the white man, or the man himself. He couldn't stand the foreboding silence and was the first man to crack.

'*Bosi* Tony… I, these men… they have accused me of…' he stammered back into silence. He looked as if panic-stricken from Tony to his *piccanin* Matabele tracker.

Both were staring at him with disconcerting menace, until Tony finally spoke. 'What… you didn't think we saw you when you fucking well brought Vusa and Mehluki up to the Msuna stockades in the ZimParks truck you drove? That was a bloody stupid fool thing to do, wasn't it?' He lapsed back into silence, still staring at the confused and deeply concerned Shona.

No, it wasn't the sight of the man, it was definitely the man himself. Tony and his smoldering angry aura intimidated Tanaka beyond belief. But with a huge effort he somehow forced himself to remain silent.

Finally, Tony turned to look at Ben, who propped his head to the side, as if trying to decide what to say.

Over the last few days he had been busy with what in essence was disseminating and receiving information across the unofficial African bush telegraph that recognized neither international boundaries nor tribal affiliations. The name Douglas Tanaka was mentioned and within a short period from across the border in Zambia, from the village of Kawaza, the home of the Kunda ironsmiths, located adjacent to the South Luangwa National Park to be precise, a font of information was forthcoming.

'Tell me, Douglas,' Ben began in Swahili, now attracting the man's full attention, 'how is your little laughing dove, your *njiwa*?'

It cracked the old man's resolve and spilled out every detail. He confessed to taking Vusa on the recce to Msuna before the attempted raid, giving some spurious explanation that he was forced to because his life was threatened. He also ratted out the Arab, Hbubari, for looting the warehouse and even helpfully gave his address in the bordering Zambian capital.

Before the week of inactivity was up, after Vusa's raid had gone terribly wrong, the Kunda ironsmiths at Vusa's warehouse damped down their kilns, packed up their tools and headed back to their village. Not long after the last tribesman left, plainclothes Criminal Investigation Department policemen, from the country's notorious CID, descended on the compound and tore the place apart looking to seize any and all valuable goods, only to find it gone.

Later that same night there was a knock at Hbubari's front door at his home in its drab Lusaka suburb. When he answered it, ten men burst in and he was surprised to see they were dressed as ZimParks rangers, having made a clandestine two-and-half-hour trip from neighboring Zimbabwe's Mana Pools National Park.

After Tanaka's tip off and confession, Tony and Ben had hastily organized the trip, commandeering two trucks and carrying it out under the guise of a ZimParks wildlife crime investigations branch operation. As Tony barged through the door he and his team realized they had only arrived just in the nick of time. The walls of Hbubari's hallway were lined with suitcases and packing crates. He was planning to slip out of Zambia with the loot that night, head up to the *entrepôt* of Burundi and drop out of sight for a while. Then when he felt the coast was clear he would fly home to Yemen, where he would disappear like a ghost in a fog, to live a life of low-key luxury.

Tony personally handcuffed Hbubari around the base of his toilet bowl and left him there, indignantly exclaiming about being confined so closely to such an unclean and unholy receptacle. Tony ignored him as he and his team formed a production line, sorting and bagging the plundered contraband. A staggering heap of rhino horns, finished and unfinished *jambiyas*, and elephant tusks were sorted through and taken to the trucks to be spirited back in to Mana Pools.

Only after crossing the invisible border for Zimbabwe near Mafuta, adjacent to the park, they alerted the Zambian authorities to inform them where they could find Hbubari.

A short time later, a pair of plainclothes CID officers showed up at Hbubari's home, briefly releasing him from around the toilet, before handcuffing him once again and bundling him into the back of an unmarked patrol car. After being processed and charged with theft and conspiring to smuggle illicit wildlife contraband at the Lusaka's Central Police Station, he was taken on the two-and-a-half-hour journey to the notorious Mukobeko Maximum Correctional Facility on the outskirts of Kabwe, in Zambia's central province. Taken from the local Lenje language, *mukobeko* meant punishment, and that is exactly what the Arab could expect to receive.

Behind its huge, plastered cinderblock walls, he was taken to a fluorescent-lit interrogation cell in the condemn section, the most secretive section in the prison. He was stripped naked and repeatedly beaten with rubber hoses until he answered the interrogator's one and only question.

When the Zambian CID raided his home to recover the produce and the rhino horn *jambiyas* that he had stolen and found nothing, he was further beaten this time with hardwood truncheons. Afterwards he was dragged to a communal cell, housing ten times the number of inmates that it was originally designed for, dumped unceremoniously unconscious just inside the door. He was lucky, as at that time due to the severe congestion, with the men packed to the rafters, half the men were standing while the others lay trying to sleep.

Douglas Tanaka had a confused expression on his dried, withered face. Several days after his arrest, he stood perplexed in his newly acquired khaki prison garb just through the barred entrance to the holding cell at the jail in the small Zimbabwean border settlement of Chirundu. He had hoped since he truthfully answered all *Bosi* Tony and his *piccanin's* questions, having snitched on everyone, the police would let him go. So he was surprised to be brought before the district magistrate, Edward Makomo, in the small courtroom in Kariba, where he was charged with conspiring to commit a wildlife crime and aiding and abetting the poaching of a specially protected species of black rhinoceros, in violation of the Endangered Species Act. He had been sentenced to five-years imprisonment. His defense had been to plead to the magistrate, 'But they are only animals.' He had received an extra two years for his lack of remorse and that ignorant assessment of what he had done.

Me and my stupid mouth, he thought as he shuffled over to sit on the cell's hardwood bench. At least he was near the border of Zambia, close to his youngest wife in Lusaka. He sighed fondly as he thought about her. But then he sat bolt upright. He had a perplexing thought, wondering due to his severely altered circumstances, if she would actually even visit him at all. *No*, he suspected, *his little laughing dove would probably fly away.*

After being away for several days having his stitches removed, his hurried clandestine trip to Lusaka, and meeting with the WWF in Harare, Tony returned to Mana Pools just before sundown. He rushed into the ranger's station, wanting to catch Glenn before he headed out for the night. But the moment he walked through the door, Glenn ambushed him.

'You won't believe what's happened?' he called excitedly from across the room. 'They found him.'

Tony looked at him blankly. 'Found who?'

'The patrol you sent into the bush, below the Msuna stockades, found two human skulls. The section head radioed us, and we contacted the police. Only a few torn items of clothing, the skulls, and assault rifles were scattered around in the bush near where you directed them to look. It was assumed that the two bodies were eaten by predators and vultures. We asked the magistrate, Edward Makomo, to intercede with the Fallen Heroes Trust, and oh how he came through.' Glenn was still buzzing from the information he had just received. 'Checked against army dental records and fingerprints lifted from the weapons, the remains have been positively identified as those belonging to Vusa, the poaching kingpin, and his lieutenant.'

'So Vusa and his henchman have been devoured and shat out throughout the valley.' Tony's smile broadened and he breathed a huge sigh of relief, not having to divulge what actually happened to the poaching kingpin. He couldn't chance telling the truth and risk the rhino being labeled under Zimbabwean law as incorrigible, needing to be put down for taking a human life. To his knowledge, Glenn had always been a stickler for following the rules.

'I thought that the bastard was going to get away with everything,' Glenn said, his steely-grey eyes glinting happily in the early-evening light as he spoke. 'But he got what he deserved. Maybe there is a God… it's divine justice.'

'Divine justice indeed,' Tony repeated, distinctly remembering the moment the bloody point of the rhino horn came bursting through Vusa's chest. 'You know this changes everything, don't you?'

Glenn nodded along knowingly. The loss and damage to the park was incalculable.

'With a warrant out for his arrest and now the confirmation that he's dead, we can go after all his Zimbabwean property, which from the official records that have been uncovered are apparently substantial.'

A smile crept across Glenn's face. 'Even so, ZimParks is going to seek restitution from the Zambian government to seize his assets there as well.'

Tony had never seen Glenn so happy. This neatly led him to what he had hurried here to discuss. He filled him in on the plans that he and the WWF came up with to organize a public ivory-and-rhino horn burning of the confiscated contraband, while also inviting the world press as leverage to pressurize the Zambian government for restitution. He added that they could use the momentum and notoriety of the smuggling kingpin's downfall to bring in sweeping reform for even tighter wildlife protection and harsher sentencing.

'Well, this calls for a celebration.' Glenn crossed the room and returned with chilled Cokes from the fridge and an expensive bottle of vintage Admirals rum he had been saving for such an occasion. He mixed them both sundowners and handed Tony his drink.

They wandered out to the deck chairs near the river just as the fiery-necked nightjars signaled the setting sun. The night was rich with the woodsy scents of river hyacinth, water lilies and glorious night-blooming jasmine. Straw-colored fruit bats swooped across the scarlet-flushed sky. Unseen creatures stirred in the tangle of trees and brush and hyraxes, the furry little relatives of elephants, screamed their nightly songs. Frogs croaked and hippos honked from the river.

In the calm, Tony thought the heat, the dust, the mosquitos, the anxiety, the injuries, it was all worth it. He couldn't help but smile when he thought about the fugitive valley prince.

That miracle of a rhino had inadvertently contributed to making the Zambezi Valley a peaceful sanctuary for himself and the other animals.

Glenn took a swig from his drink and gazed toward the water. 'You've done a helluva job patrolling and protecting what's left of the wildlife in the corridor,' he said a little wistfully, 'Pity, with your departure, it will soon go unprotected.'

'Oh, I don't think you need to worry,' Tony answered cryptically. He pitied any poacher who now went into the corridor and was unlucky enough to cross paths with The Last Rhino.

That was one rhino he was more than happy to leave in the Zambezi Valley.

OTHER BOOKS BY THE AUTHOR

African Series:

The Last Rhino is a prequel to *White Gold* in my African series, the events in this story take place just prior to the start of Tony Campbell's next African Wildlife Thriller. If you enjoyed *The Last Rhino* you may like to follow on with *White Gold*.

Book 1: **Scars of the Leopard**

Book 2: **White Gold**

Book 3: **African Lion**

CONTACT ME
Get personalized book information and up-to-date news about my works:
DavidMarkQuigley.com

Be the first to know about new releases, awesome giveaways and news by signing up for the VIP mailing list: **books@davidmarkquigley.com**

REVIEWS
Did you enjoy this book? If so, I would love to hear about it. Honest reviews help readers find the right book for their needs. To leave a review, please head to *The Last Rhino*'s Amazon page, scroll to the bottom of the page under "More about the author", and select "Write a customer review".

I hope you enjoy reading this book as much as I did writing it. It has been a pleasure having you as one of my readers. Thank you!

Did you know that a portion of your proceeds is seamlessly donated to wildlife causes around the world? To find out more, please turn to the next page.

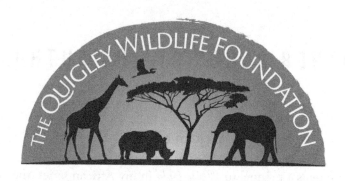

Save the Rhino International[1] estimates that almost 10,000 rhinos have been lost to poaching in the last decade. Similarly, the International Union for the Conservation of Nature (IUCN)[2] reports that, as of 2021, Africa's elephants are now considered critically endangered.

> *"Wildlife needs all the help that it can get. That's what resonates with me the most and why I chose to start this Foundation."* – David Mark Quigley

The Quigley Wildlife Foundation
The Quigley Wildlife Foundation is a registered 501(c)3 non-profit organisation registered in Florida that donates to wildlife causes around the world.

The foundation is comprised of five Directors, each with diverse international backgrounds and wide-net-reach to various organizations and charities around the world.

David Mark Quigley
Author of the African series. Born in New Zealand, traveled and lived extensively around the world.

Rhonda J Brenner
Born and bred Floridian. Incidentally, the author's wife.

Robert Luke Noble
Originally hailing from Michigan, now a resident of Naples, Florida.

Terry Dorval
Born in Haiti, now a resident of Naples, Florida.

Doris Sloan Moon
Born and bred Floridian.

With your purchase of any of my books you are seamlessly donating to a worthy cause, as a portion of all proceeds for my books goes to Wildlife Preservation. Thank you for your part in protecting wildlife!

If you would like more information about the foundation, I would love to hear from you. Please email: David Mark Quigley
dmq@davidmarkquigley.com

1. www.savetherhino.org/whino-info/poaching-stats/

2. www.iucn.org/news/species/202103/african-elephant-species-now-endangered-and-critically-endangered-iucn-red-list